TRAIL OF A HARD MAN

TRAIL OF
A HARD MAN

by

Chuck Tyrell

Dales Large Print Books
Long Preston, North Yorkshire,
BD23 4ND, England.

British Library Cataloguing in Publication Data.

Tyrell, Chuck
    Trail of a hard man.

    A catalogue record of this book is
    available from the British Library

    ISBN   978-1-84262-561-3 pbk

First published in Great Britain in 2006 by Robert Hale Limited

Cover illustration © Gordon Crabb by arrangement with
Alison Eldred

Published in Large Print 2007 by arrangement with
Robert Hale Ltd.

Dales Large Print is an imprint of Library Magna Books Ltd.

Printed and bound in Great Britain by
T.J. (International) Ltd., Cornwall, PL28 8RW

CHAPTER 1

I'm known as a hard man. But even hard men ride careful on the outlaw trail. Not that I'm on the wrong side of John Law, though some say I am. And I never claimed any different, not being prone to talk a lot.

Maybe I got that outlaw image because I am hard. Never take guff from any man. Not that I look for it, but trouble just seems to come my way naturally.

After the sun painted its version of heaven's glory across the clear Utah sky, the night got black as a Ute warrior's insides. No moon. Ol' Buck slowed to a careful walk through the darkness. He naturally stepped quiet, being wild born and mountain bred. I smelled the Colorado first, a fragrance of wet earth and green leaves you don't find in the desert. A little later, I heard the water moving along with the full-throated chuckle of a grown river.

Then Buck stopped.

I froze, too, breathing shallow. The horse pricked his ears toward the mountain side of the trail, so I shucked my Winchester and piled off the downhill side. I liked that horse, but few weapons – not even big Sharps

7

buffalo guns – could shoot clear through a big horse like my buckskin.

I could hear only silence, like nothing was breathing, so I just stood there with my rifle ready.

'Ness Havelock? That you, Ness?'

I'd heard that calm, low-pitched voice before. But I couldn't place it, so I didn't answer. A man can get shot in the dark by speaking up too soon.

'Guess it must be you, Ness,' the voice continued. 'You ain't shooting, and you ain't running. It's Isom Dart. I got coffee on.'

Isom Dart, the outlaw mail. If a body wanted to talk to anyone on the outlaw trail, he just told Isom, and the message got delivered. That black man had a mighty good reputation. I led the buckskin in the direction of his receding footsteps.

Isom sure knew how to pick a camp. He'd chosen a spot in an arroyo that took water into the Colorado after a rain. Right now, the bottom was bone dry. The slight breeze wafted the fragrance of coffee up the cut and into the mountains. A rider on the trail wouldn't be able to smell it. And that fire – I could've covered the whole thing with my hat.

Dart held up the pot and I stuck out my tin mug. We sat drinking coffee and savoring the night for a while.

'They's trouble abrew down in Little

Colorado country,' he said after a bit. 'Word come over the line that Roland Prince's looking for you. Says he needs help.'

I had my thoughts fixed on a pretty Spanish girl by the name of Margarita San Antonio Pilar y Guerrero. Rita. But now...

'Owe Prince a lot,' I said.

'Heard about Sonora. I know you don't need no advice, Ness, but somethin' about this don't set right. You need to ride wide awake.'

'Thanks for the coffee, Isom. And the message. I'd stay for breakfast, but I've got a feather bed waiting in Moab.'

Isom looked at me with those sad brown eyes of his. 'The word's out, Ness. And a feather bed's as good a place to bushwhack a man as any.'

Isom was far behind me when I topped the bluff above Moab. The Mormon side of the river was quiet. Few windows showed lights. But on the heathen side, things were just getting warmed up. Whoops and hollers drifted out to meet me when I was still a good mile off. I couldn't help but grin. I rubbed a hand through a two-day growth of beard. A beer and a shave, that's what I needed. Still, I slipped the thong off the hammer of my six-gun as I rode across the wooden bridge over the Colorado.

Some folks thought I wore my Colt peculiar, high on my left hip, butt forward. I got that style from my brother, Garet, a no-give lawman. Wearing my iron like that, all I had to do was slip my hand around that walnut grip, yank it out, and start shootin'.

A lantern burned in front of the livery barn. In its pool of light, an old man sat reading. He squinted up at me as I rode up. 'One stall left, mister, back on the right. Hay's in the loft and oats in the bin in the corner. Fifty cents.'

I put four bits on the upturned palm and led the buckskin to the last open stall. I rubbed him down, forked his hay, and put two quarts of oats in his feed box. When I got back to the door, the old-timer was still reading his book, mouthing each word through his white beard.

'Always did like a good book,' I said to make conversation. 'Makes a man consider some.'

He put a finger on a word to hold his place. 'You got something to say, stranger, get it said. If not, just amble along, so's I can get on with my Blackstone.'

'Blackstone, is it? Writes a good book on law. Tell me, is there anyone in town I should watch out for?'

'Jigger Baines is here. And J.T. Carr is down from Wyoming.'

'What's a lawman doing here?'

'Ain't heard. Mebbe he's after Ruel Gatlin. The boy shot a bartender up to Casper

10

the other day.'

At the name Gatlin, my scars itched. I had three, one for each of the Gatlin boys, though Lawrence Gatlin put two bullets in me while I was killing his brothers.

Back then, Telluride was just a swarm of canvas and clapboard shacks and miners' tents with a long line of saloons. My Gatlin trouble started in the Lucky Seven. While I'm not a hard drinker, I like to cut the dust with a glass of good rye. And the ride through the high Colorado mountains from Ouray to Telluride had been a long one.

The Gatlins had the town pretty well buffaloed, but I never been one to move just because someone leaned on me. The main street boasted one two-storey frame building, the Watson House, the bottom floor a saloon, and the upper one full of rooms with women's names on them.

I'd no more than bellied up against the smooth wood of the beautiful bar in the Watson House, gotten a glass of good rye, and started to salute myself in the mirror, than a big muscle of a man come in the front door. I push at six feet, but he stood a good two inches above me and weighed maybe fifty pounds over my one eighty.

He dressed fine, but his bloodshot eyes didn't look the dandy. He reminded me of a big old longhorn bull I flushed popping brush for Charlie Goodnight down in Texas.

11

I just left that old bull there, pawing in the brush. I'da done the same with the man, too, if he'd a given me the chance.

I turned my back to the door, putting my left hip against the bar so the butt of my Colt was only an inch away from my right hand. In the mirror I watched the big man come. He wanted me and no one else. He stopped spraddle-legged about five feet behind me and growled, 'Hey, you.'

I turned a little to look at him.

'Telluride don't have no room for drifters. Drink up and ride on.' He balanced forward on his toes, glaring at me.

I kept my voice low. 'I don't see a badge on you, mister.'

His face went red. 'Gatlins are law here. I'm Mort Gatlin and I say you leave. Now!'

With my left hand, I flicked that good rye whiskey into Mort Gatlin's eyes. With my right, I plucked out my Colt and whacked the side of his head hard just above the ear with its seven-and-a-half-inch barrel. He went down and stayed there.

'You'd better ride, mister.' The bartender's voice was low and not unfriendly. 'Mort Gatlin's got two brothers, and one of 'em's bigger'n him. All three are hell raisers with guns.'

'Thanks, but I've got a hankering to sleep in a good bed. Know where I could get a little rest?'

'Ma Blaisdell's got a boarding-house down the street about a mile. Just a simple house, but it's first rate.'

'Obliged.' I tossed him a coin for the rye and the conversation. He tossed it back.

'Keep your money. 'Twas worth it to see Mort Gatlin hit the floor.'

'Well, once he wakes up, he'll be wanting to know who buffaloed him. Tell him Johannes Havelock's gone to Ma Blaisdell's for a rest. Tell him it'd be healthy to let Mr. Havelock ride out peaceful.'

The bartender grinned. 'I'll tell him, but I don't think he'll listen.'

'Then I'll have to read him some of the gospel according to Sam Colt.' I stepped around Gatlin's inert body and walked out. I found Ma Blaisdell's place right where the bartender had said.

'Havelock,' Mort Gatlin's bull voice roared. 'You've lived too long.'

By the time his shout died away, I was wide awake and catfootin' down the hallway to the back door, boots in my left hand and gun in my right. I pulled the boots on and stepped out into the bright Colorado day. Slipping around behind the line of buildings, I came out on the main street about a hundred feet from the three big men standing in front of Ma Blaisdell's. I holstered my six-gun and said, 'You boys looking for me?'

Mort went for his gun. I plucked mine

out, took a quick step to my right, and shot Mort through the left shirt pocket. The other Gatlins were no more'n a split second behind Mort, but I still managed to get a bullet into big Steve before the smaller one, Lawrence, put lead into me.

The force of his bullet turned me around and I fell. Scrambling across the hard ground, Gatlin bullets kicking chunks of dirt at me, I fetched up against the hitching post, gun aimed at Lawrence Gatlin's head. Then I shifted and shot him in the stomach. The biggest Gatlin sprawled at the edge of the porch and lay still.

I caught a movement from the corner of my eye and was already rolling when a second bullet plowed into me. I'd mistaken Mort Gatlin for dead. Now I was hit and hit bad. I could barely see Mort through the red haze that settled over my eyes, but almost by instinct, I triggered off a round that tore a chunk from his head.

I wiped my sleeve across my face, trying to get the blood out of my eyes. In the distance, I heard a gun firing and felt the burn of a bullet across my shoulder. Squinting, I made out Lawrence Gatlin, one hand on his bloody stomach, trying to thumb back the hammer of his Colt for another shot. My bullet caught him in the throat, slamming him against Ma Blaisdell's front porch. His hands clawed at the wall, leaving streaks of red on the white clap-boards.

Then all was silent. Smoke drifted down the street. I heaved myself to my feet and reloaded, scooped my hat from the ground, and staggered to my horse. I heard the murmur of folks gatherin' as I rode out of Telluride toward Utah.

I made it to Moab, but just barely. I went to Myra Beck's place, and she pulled me through. Two weeks in a feather bed with plenty of care got me back on my feet. Myra was a widow, her man killed by Utes about fifteen years earlier. I guess she's as close to a mother as I ever had. Mine died in the Indian Nations while I was being born.

When the old geezer at the livery stable told me Ruel, the fourth and youngest Gatlin, was in town, the old scars started hurting again. I hesitated for a moment, then made my way toward the sounds of revelry.

The saloons stood out among the dark buildings lining the street, two on the south side, one on the north. At the door of the Lamplight, I turned to look across the street at The Pig's Ear and the Buckhorn. The tinny tunes from the pianos mixed, and once in a while, a wild whoop or a shrill laugh wafted across the street as the girls and their customers sparred in the yellow light of coal-oil lamps.

Inside, the Lamplight was dark enough

15

that a man's eyes didn't have to adjust much coming in out of the night. A woman sat at the piano in a far corner, playing soothing music. The click of a ball against the roulette wheel's dividers was the loudest sound in the room.

Ed Snedeker stood behind his bar, a contented look on his round, red face. His hair was parted precisely in the middle and greased down to cling to his round skull. Ed knew more about what was going on up and down the Trail than anyone, save Isom Dart. He moved down in front of me.

'Rye?'

I nodded.

'J.T. Carr's been asking about you.'

'I'm here.'

Ed slid a shot glass of good rye down the bar. It stopped in front of me without a drop spilled. As I picked up the glass, Carr walked in.

He paused just inside, then sauntered over. He put both hands on the bar so I wouldn't misunderstand.

'Hear you're headed south,' he said.

'I am.'

'Mind if I ride along?'

'Suit yourself. I'm leaving first light. After a drink or two, I'll head for a good night's rest in a feather bed.'

'I'd sleep lightly, if I was you. Some'd feel better if you never got to Arizona. Sid Lyle's talking about dealing with Ness Havelock. Permanent. And he's got help.'

'Who?'

'Junior Willis, Kid Kilgallen, Nate Blackthorn, and Carl Jaeger,' Carr said. He turned to go, then looked back. 'Oh, Ruel Gatlin is in town. He wants you, too.'

I paid for the rye and left. On my way to Myra Beck's place, a flicker in the shadows caught my eye. Later, as I was ready to settle into that soft feather tick, I remembered the movement. Out of caution, I bunched up the bedclothes to look something like a body, took my Colt in hand, and put myself in the far corner with a blanket.

A shotgun blast and the sound of shattering glass woke me instantly. I started to shoot back, then chuckled under my breath. Someone had just shot Ness Havelock dead.

CHAPTER 2

A long-eared mule is a sizeable chunk of hell after a few hours in the saddle. I'd sworn never to ride a mule, but there I was. I was dead and buried. And with two days and nearly eighty miles behind me, the only ones who knew different were me, Myra Beck, and J.T. Carr.

Ordinarily I fancy gray duds, because gray blends with the lie of just about any land. But I left my good gray stuff in Moab to be buried.

Now I rode a motherless mule and wore a floppy excuse for a hat. My shirt, once maroon, had hardly any color, and instead of gray whipcord trousers, I wore faded brown corduroy ones. My boots weren't black and shiny either. They were scuffed cavalry cast-offs that came almost to my knees, and my pant legs tucked inside them.

I had my Colt, safe in my waistband beneath the tail of that once-maroon shirt, yet I was a different man. I usually sat straight in the saddle, but on this old mule, I slouched and bobbed, swaying with his gait. And with a five-day growth of beard on my face, I doubt if two people in the entire territory of Arizona could've recognized me.

Tomorrow would put me in Mexican Hat, about ten miles from the Arizona border. Tonight I made a dry camp under a crystal-clear sky. Every star stood out, each trying to out-twinkle the next. Off a ways, I could hear the mule cropping at stubble. He was a trail-wise booger who'd let me know if anything unusual came along.

At dawn, the mule's snort woke me. My hand went to my Colt, thumb cocking the hammer. The mule stood at full attention, jack-rabbit ears pointing south. Then I heard the sound of pounding hoofs. Someone had come far and fast, and the horse was fading, his stride rough and uneven.

I faced the rider, gun in hand, when he topped the rise south of me. Sweat darkened the little grulla mustang's color to gunmetal, and lather slopped to the ground with each uneven stride. The eyes of the youngster on the mouse-colored horse showed the whites like a frightened colt.

I put the gun away and picked up my Winchester, automatically checking the cartridge in the chamber. I eared the hammer back to half-cock.

The boy held onto the saddle horn with both hands, and when he pulled the mustang up, I noticed a dark stain running from beneath his right arm down his flimsy shirt and onto his pants. The grulla stopped and stood spraddle-legged, head down.

'Please, mister,' the boy said, his voice trembling, 'sure could use some help.' Then his eyeballs turned up and he toppled off the horse. I just barely got a hand on him to break his fall. What I saw made me more than a little mad. The youngster'd been whipped. His back would carry the scars to the grave. Under his right arm, the whip had torn flesh from his ribs. The wound needed sewing, but that had to wait because riders came boiling over the rise. The man out front rode a big bay, thick through the shoulders and hindquarters. The man was big, too, and around his left shoulder coiled the black snake of a bullwhip.

As I walked out to meet him, pulling the hammer of my Winchester to full cock, the bay came plunging at me full stride. I stood my ground, the muzzle of my rifle following the big man's belly. He hung back on the reins, bringing the bay to a sliding stop.

'Thanks for catching that runaway, stranger,' the big man said. 'Peterson,' he called, and a skinny rider with his hat pulled down around his jug ears broke out of the pack and raced his mount toward us. 'Load that kid on the spare horse. We'll not bother this gentleman any longer.'

'Peterson,' I said, 'you lay a hand on that boy you or your boss's dead.'

That confused the rider and made the big

man mad. 'Mister, I hope you know whom you're threatening,' he said. 'I'm Judge Harlow Wilson.'

'Leave the boy be.'

'Look. You're outnumbered. Don't be a fool.'

'Now, Wilson, there's only one of you, and I'll kill you if anyone touches that boy.'

The black hole in the muzzle of my Winchester took big bites out of his courage. He opened his mouth twice, but no sound came out. Finally he wrenched the bay horse around and took off back down the trail toward Mexican Hat, his men tailing along behind. I had a feeling I'd not seen the last of that man.

The boy lay as he'd fallen, breathing shallow. I put him face down on my bedroll and went to work. It took the better part of an hour to get the blood-crusted shirt out of the slashes in his back and to sew the flap of flesh dangling under his arm. I used a lot of whiskey, hoping the wounds wouldn't fester. I got my only clean shirt on the boy, big though it was. He remained unconscious, and I didn't like his pale color or the shallow way he breathed. But along toward evening, he opened his eyes.

'Thanks, mister.' His voice was barely a whisper. 'Sure feels good. Ain't had no help for a long time.'

'Where's your folks?'

'Ain't got none.'

'What's Wilson to you?'

The boy hesitated, then said, 'After my folks died of the diphtheria, Judge Wilson took me in. He takes in kids 'cause he wants extra hands what don't cost nothing. He's got five kids right now, 'cept I run off. He likes to hurt. Every horse on the place's scared of him. The kids are, too.'

The boy's face went red and sweat come out on his brow. I felt his forehead. He burned with fever.

His talking got wild after that. He shouted and pleaded. Then, about midnight, he slept, or maybe he lost consciousness.

Since there was nothing I could do for him, I slept for a while. The stars were still out when I woke, but something felt wrong. I looked at the boy. His white face was turned to the sky. I knew before I put a hand to his cold forehead that he was dead.

Deep down, I felt a fury building. Harlow Wilson was going to pay. I swore to it as I mounted that spiny-backed mule and turned his head toward Saint Johns. The grulla mustang fell in behind of its own accord.

What would've been five days on my buckskin, took a week on that mule. But he was just as fresh when we rode into Saint Johns as he'd been when we left Mexican Hat. Me, the mule, and the grulla mustang sported a thick layer of trail dust. It was a toss-up as to whether I'd take a bath first, or get a drink. I settled on a bath.

I walked into the barber shop that flanked Solomon's Mercantile.

'Bath?' the barber asked.

I nodded.

'Fifty cents.'

I paid, took the scrawny towel and cake of yellow lye soap, and headed for the barrels of hot water out back. Thirty minutes of scrubbing and rinsing made me feel brand new, ready to get a look at the lie of the land.

Shucking my long-barrel Winchester .44-40 from the saddle scabbard, I mounted to go to the livery stable a hundred yards back down the street. Saint Johns was a good-sized town, yet there was hardly anyone to be seen. Even the windows gave off uneasy stares. And with no one at the livery stable, I helped myself to the fodder and oats. After giving the mule and the grulla rubdowns, I checked my Colt and the Winchester and walked up the street.

Saint Johns was divided in three: the Mormons on the hill, the Mexicans down by the river, and everybody else over here. The town boasted two saloons, the Longhorn and the Fox and Hounds. I decided to try the Fox and Hounds first.

Inside, the saloon was like any other, bar

along the right-hand wall, four tables down the left. Two cowboys quietly played cards in the back of the room. The barkeep stood stolidly behind a plank of oak, his expression neutral.

'What'll it be?'

'Beer.'

The barkeep slid the brew down the bar, foam slopping over the brim. He followed with a cloth, wiping the flecks of foam from the polished oak plank.

'Passing through?' he asked.

'Looks like a friendly town. I may stay a while.'

'Punch cows?'

'Some.'

'Preston Hanks's looking for men. You might give him a try.'

'What kind of spread does he run?'

'The Claymore runs about fifteen thousand head up toward the Blues. He's got Englishmen backing him.'

The bartender took another swipe at the oak plank. He sidled a little closer, put his elbows on the bar, and spoke in low confidential tones. 'Hanks's had trouble lately. He wants men who can handle their guns better than most.'

I lifted my beer mug to the barkeep in a salute, chugged the brew, and left him standing there polishing oak.

Now I knew that Hanks had trouble and

Roland Prince had trouble, and that Harlow Wilson's Pitchfork meant trouble if it was bringing in fifty thousand beeves.

Outside, the weather was hot, and Ness Havelock – him a dead man – was the only thing moving on Saint Johns' Commerce Street. I walked out of the saloon, crossed the street, and went in the Longhorn. I got two steps in the door and a big voice growled, 'You want to drink at the Fox and Hounds, cowboy, then just trot yourself back over there. Only decent people drink at the Longhorn.'

I turned slow and looked at the owner of that voice.

'You talking to me?' I walked straight at the man, who stood three or four inches taller than me.

'Yeah. Get out.'

'Well now,' I said, leaning the Winchester against a table. 'Suppose you throw me out?' And I put my weight behind a stiff right that splatted against the big man's face like a mallet smacking a side of beef. His eyes got kinda red and I could see he was a brawler, but the boxing Sergeant Kelly taught me and my brother Garet would even out the odds if I could keep his hands off me.

'Go get him, Jerry,' urged a bystander. Jerry came, arms pumping like pistons. I stepped out of his way and mashed his ear with a solid left. He lost his balance and

25

plowed through two tables – broke the legs off one and cracked the other with the crown of his head.

'Jerry,' I said. 'You quiet down, and I'll let you off.'

He came off the floor and smashed me on the cheek with a huge right fist. The inside of my mouth crushed against my teeth and I tasted the smoky salt of my own blood.

Jerry swung at me again, and clobbered me in the forehead, which sent my head whipping back and forth like my neck was rubber.

He reached out and gathered me into a bear hug. I forced my elbows against his thick chest, and tried to make breathing room. Now I'm no kid. At 180, with much of that weight in my arms and shoulders, I can lift and pull with the best of them. But Jerry was handling me like I was a child. He shifted his grip lower and tighter. I had to do something, else I'd suffocate or my ribs would crack.

I couldn't get a knee into Jerry's crotch, he was wise to that. So I raised a leg and scraped the sole of my old cavalry boot all the way down the big man's shin and stomped as hard as I could on his left instep.

The bear hug loosened a little, and I got an arm out. I hooked my fingers across Jerry's eyeballs. He hollered and clapped a hand to his face, and I slugged him in the back of the neck with my clasped hands. He went to his knees, a hand still covering his eyes. Then I brought a knee into his face and he bellowed as blood splattered. With every ounce of my strength, I hooked a right that landed right behind Jerry's ear. He dropped like a shot dogie. I pulled my Colt from my waistband with a sore right hand.

I motioned to big Jerry's buddies. 'Now, if you men will back up against the wall, we'll get to the bottom of this misunderstanding.'

Jerry struggled on to all fours. Blood dripped from the end of his nose to puddle on the floor. He swiped at it with the back of a big hand. Somehow he got to his feet and stood there, swaying back and forth like a mad grizzly, taking it all in – me with my Colt in my hand, and his friends against the wall with their hands clasped behind their heads.

Slowly he turned until he faced me straight on and for a long moment he just stood there and glared. A mouse running across the floor would've sounded like a moose. Then he grinned and stuck out a big hand. 'You'll do,' he said. 'I'm Jerry Simpson. Put 'er there.'

I did.

Suddenly the place was a bedlam. Everyone bought drinks for everybody else. The house even bought a round. When things quieted down, I found myself at a table in a dark corner with Simpson.

'If you're a mind, I'd like to hear your moniker,' he said.

'I've been called Johnny,' I said, using the name I'd worn before Rita christened me Ness.

Simpson grinned. 'Johnny it is. You planning to stick around? Or just passing through?'

'They say the Blues has good places where a man could settle down, kind of out and away from everything. I thought I'd drift over near Escudilla and have a look. But I don't want trouble. Anyone fighting over that land?'

'Not exactly.' Simpson's face got serious. 'But there's trouble around.'

'Trouble?'

'An outfit called the Pitchfork's herding fifty thousand head of cattle this way from Texas,' Simpson said.

'Who'll get hurt?'

'Preston Hanks, for one. He runs white-faced cattle over toward the Blues and don't want Texas longhorns mixing with them. Can't say's I blame him, even if he and my boss don't agree on things.'

'What's his problem?'

Simpson looked at me like he wasn't sure he should be talking so much, me being a stranger and all. But he kept at it. 'The boss,

Roland Prince, has a couple or three problems. Sometimes Hanks runs his cattle on to our grazing land, and our dogies use part of a Spanish grant held by Mexes named Pilar. God knows what's gonna happen when Pitchfork cows get here.'

'Are the Mexicans pushing?'

'No, but they run sheep on that range in the wintertime.'

'I heard there was sheep trouble a year or so ago.'

'Loren Buchard's boy Rafe done that. He shot Garet Havelock that ex-lawman who raises horses over on Silver Creek. Rafe's in Yuma prison now.'

'Prince gonna push the Mexicans?'

'I think his main worry's Hanks. 'Cause Hanks hired Sid Lyle about a month ago, and Lyle brought four of his own rannies.

'Boss sent to El Paso for Garet Havelock's younger brother Ness. Says he's a hard man. But now it seems Havelock got himself killed up to Moab.'

'I know the place.'

'Anyways, there's been no word from Havelock. But the boss keeps saying "Ness'll come. Hell or high water," he says, "Ness'll come".'

I got that prickly feeling again. Something wasn't right. 'Thanks for the drink,' I said, and stood up. I shook Simpson's big paw, grabbed my rifle, and strode toward the door of the Longhorn. I paused for a moment, then stepped through quickly. Nothing stirred on Commerce Street.

About halfway across the bridge toward Mexican town, I saw dust boiling up as horses raced toward town from the west. I hung my elbows over the bridge railing and waited to see who was in such an all-fired hurry.

From under the brim of my floppy hat, I saw four riders flanking a buckboard pulled by a pair of lathered horses. I pulled the hat down over my eyes and leaned against the rail to let the rig and its flankers roar by. I recognized one of the riders, Ace Cruger, a tough man and a good one. And I knew the men in the buckboard. Roland Prince was one. Not the Roland Prince I knew – a big hearty man, burned by the sun, hard and fit from countless hours in the saddle. But a Roland Prince who was pale and drawn, who clung to the back of the seat.

Harlow Wilson drove the buckboard, but he didn't seem to recognize me.

When the buckboard pulled up in front of the Longhorn, I saw why Prince was different. Two men helped him from the rig. Another handed him a pair of crutches. Through narrowed eyes, I watched him struggle through the door, followed by Wilson. Things weren't what I'd figured.

The Mexican side of Saint Johns showed

signs of life. Kids hollered from behind the adobe buildings that lined the street. Chickens scratched in the dust for sprigs of green and unwary bugs. Mongrel dogs shaded up wherever they could find a comfortable spot.

Only one sign graced the street, so I had no trouble finding the cantina. Inside, it was dark and musty. A wooden table with a stack of empty bottles stood off to one side with a case behind it. Only one drink served – mescal. Shriveled limes squatted on the table's corner next to a well-honed butcher knife. A pottery bowl of salt sat in the middle of the table next to a stack of cloudy glasses.

A Mexican man stepped in from behind the serape hanging in the back door.

'Mescal, *por favor,*' I said.

'*Sí, señor.*' He filled a large glass about half full of clear liquor and pushed it across the table. With a swift chop of the butcher knife, he bisected a lime, shoving one half at me and keeping the other. The bottle he used didn't come from the case. That should have warned me.

I licked the knuckle of my left hand, dipped it in the bowl of salt, knocked back half of the mescal and squeezed lime juice into my mouth. I sucked the salt off my hand, and drank the rest of the mescal.

The Mexican smiled. I smiled back.

That's the last thing I remember until I came to with a razor-sharp blade pricking my neck.

CHAPTER 3

'Gently, *señor*,' a big Mexican warned. 'You are the man they call Johnny in Ciudad Juarez. Is that not correct?'

I nodded, his cold blade still at my throat.

'I thought so.' The Mexican sheathed the knife and whipped the black kerchief from his face to reveal a wide grin. He thrust out a big hand. *'Perdon* for the extra in your mescal, *amigo.'*

I scowled. *'Amigo?'*

'Ricardo sends his greetings, *señor.'*

'By who?'

'By *nosotros*, Emilio Velasquez.' The hand extended again. I reached up, grabbed it, and hauled myself upright. Dizzy, I put a hand to the wall to steady myself. 'Ricardo Rodriguez? Aah, yes, he spoke of you. Said you were a good man in a fight. Who do you fight for now?'

'Don Fernando Alfonso de Pilar y Aquilar was a friend of my sainted father – God rest his soul. I cannot stand by and see the Pilars pushed from their land.' Velasquez looked at me with hard eyes. 'Will you ride to the rancho with me?'

A ride to Rancho Pilar would put me face

33

to face with Rita, but I nodded. 'My mule is in the livery stable.'

'I have a horse for you,' Velasquez replied, and led me out the rear entrance. Two horses stood in a small pole corral. One was Buck.

'Nice looking buckskin,' I said.

Velasquez grinned. 'The horse came down the Trail to Alma from Utah. They said you might need him.'

I whistled and Buck came at a run, showering clods and dirt in a stiff-legged sliding halt, his nose flat up against my chest. Guess he missed me as much as I missed him.

My gunbelt hung from the saddle horn, so I took it off, cinched it around my hips, and put the Colt in its familiar spot high on my left hip. I shoved my Winchester into its scabbard, mounted the buckskin, and we rode out – me in my faded clothes, floppy hat, and hand-me-down cavalry boots, and Velasquez in his black leather breeches and short black Mexican jacket with gleaming silver conchos.

We passed Concho at sunset, and reached Rancho Pilar's main gate after dark. My hand went to the butt of my Colt as I heard the click-click of cocking shotgun hammers. Velasquez put a hand on my arm.

'*Soy Emilio Velasquez*,' he said to the rancho's guard. '*Mi compañero es Señor Johnny. El es muy conocido en Ciudad Juarez.*'

34

'Welcome, *señor*,' the voice said. 'My name is Jaime Roca. Salvador Espanza is my mother's cousin.'

'Salvador's a good man, the best.' That was true. Salvador stood by me in the deserts of Sonora, along with Roland Prince. Luckily, we were all still alive.

'Thank you, *señor*. Come in, Don Fernando awaits.'

A shadow in the dark opened the gate. After we passed through, I heard a bar clunk down, relocking it. With men like Jaime Roca on watch, the rancho was safer. Few fighting men could match these tough *vaqueros*. I'd fought alongside them before.

The hacienda was long and low, made of adobe and pine poles. A shaft of light spread across the beaten earth of the front yard. Outlined in the glow was the woman who had turned my world upside down. 'Welcome, Emilio.' Her voice was low, with a timbre like the soft sound of a good bronze bell. 'Father is waiting in the study.' My breath caught in my throat.

When I'd ridden away from Rancho Pilar a year and a half ago, I'd vowed to forget this woman. I hadn't been able to.

She looked regal, as if she'd just stepped from one of those paintings you see in New Orleans. Her eyes were wide, large and brown. Her skin glowed gold in the light of the lamps and her raven hair cascaded down her back from a high Spanish comb to slightly below her waist. I stared. I couldn't help it.

Emilio Velasquez led me down the hallway to the room where Don Fernando waited.

'*Señor*. It has been too long since we have seen you.' The Don extended a slim, fine-boned hand. I took it and found surprising strength in the grip.

'Don Fernando,' I said. 'Time has treated you well.'

'Will you join me in a glass of Jerez?'

'Thank you, *patron*. I will.'

'And for you, Don Emilio?'

'*Por favor*.'

The wine was bold and sweet, with the full flavor of grape carefully preserved – a good way to start serious conversation.

The massive door opened and Rita swept into the room with a tray of delicacies. Deep fried tortillas, steamed jalapeño peppers, little dishes of chilli and beef, mounds of pinto beans, boiled, mashed and refried with plenty of lard, accompanied by sourdough biscuits with sweet desert honey.

'Sourdough biscuits?' I asked.

'*Si*,' she said. 'I learned to make them from my very good friend Laura Havelock, who lives at Rancho H-Cross on Silver Creek. Perhaps you know her?'

Before I could answer, the Don said, 'And you remember my daughter Margarita.' Then to her, 'The *señor* has returned, *querida*.'

'I'm sorry but I do not remember you, *señor.*' Her voice crackled like ice.

I fumbled with my floppy hat.

'The *señor* blushes,' she said, mocking me again.

'Rita, you must not taunt our guest,' said Don Fernando. She swept from the room, and my heart went with her. I couldn't help it.

Ordinarily I steer shy of women, but Rita had something different – her spirit glowed as if from an internal fire. But she was the daughter of a Spanish Don, and I was the son of a Texas Ranger and his Cherokee wife. She was so far out of reach...

Don Fernando refilled our glasses. 'Perhaps you wonder why I had Don Emilio find you and bring you here,' he said. 'Let me tell you of the situation, as much as I can. The rest, I'm afraid you must discover for yourself.' The silver-haired Don settled himself into his leather chair.

'The year was mostly peaceful,' said Don Fernando. 'We had our grants of land, the *Mormonas* farmed, the lawless kept mostly to the foothills of the Blues. And when they came to town, it was to Round Valley, where Gus Snyder ruled.

'Good men like Loren Buchard, Preston Hanks, and Roland Prince ran cattle on public land, separating their stock at roundup time. Then trouble seemed to start when Hanks bought white-face cattle, Herefords, I think they are called.'

I turned to the Don. 'Did anyone new come to this area before the trouble started?'

Don Fernando furrowed his brow. 'Many drift in. Few stay. Many make trouble. Harlow Wilson, for example, came with his riders. Wilson owns the Pitchfork outfit. He says fifty thousand cows will soon come into Apache County.'

Harlow Wilson's name brought bitter bile to the back of my throat. 'Was there a youngster with Wilson's bunch? A blond boy, twelve, thirteen years old?'

'I saw such a boy, but he was only one of several,' the Don said. 'We heard the youngster had escaped.'

'He got away all right,' I said through clenched teeth. 'Wilson caught the boy in Mexican Hat. Whipped him again and left him tied to a wagon wheel. The youngster got loose and bolted. He died at my camp, and I buried him in Mexican Hat. His mustang is in the livery stable. It wears a Pitchfork brand.'

'I saw the boy,' Velasquez said. 'He was a good youth. He cannot go unavenged. As long as Harlow Wilson occupies God's earth, Emilio Velasquez walks on his shadow ... after you, of course.'

'One more thing happened,' Don Fernando said. 'Shortly before trouble came to our land, Roland Prince was shot from ambush. Luckily, he was not killed, but he cannot use his legs well now. The ambush was on Pilar land, and perhaps he thinks one of our *vaqueros* did it. Of course, that is not true.'

'Have you spoken to my brother of your problems?'

'Both Miguel and Rita have been to Silver Creek several times. Garet Havelock knows of our trouble. In fact, he suggested we send for you. But when we got word to Don Emilio, we found that Roland Prince had already requested your help.

'*Señor* Garet and *Señora* Laura have a fine son. They named him Beowulf....' The Don lost words for a moment. He took a deep breath. 'We need your help now as we did in the past. May we rely upon you once more, *señor*?'

Unanswered questions still bothered me. 'Why do you suppose Preston Hanks is hiring gunhands? I can see your problem with Roland Prince, but why's Preston Hanks on Roland's back?'

'I think Prince and Wilson have an understanding. Wilson's riders drink at the Longhorn. So do Prince's,' the Don said.

'That doesn't add up to an agreement.'

'True. However, I have never heard of a Pitchfork rider fighting with one from the

RP Connected. It always seems to be Claymore men who fight,' said Don Fernando.

'Claymore?'

'Yes. Hanks's brand. A cross on its side, a long horizontal line with a shorter vertical one. A Claymore is a double-handed sword.'

'A lazy cross. A Pitchfork fits right over a lazy cross. Are you sure the Pitchfork's bringing fifty thousand critters?' I asked.

'No one knows,' said Velasquez. 'And I agree that the Pitchfork fits perfectly over a Claymore.'

The whole situation puzzled me, and my confusion must have shown.

'There are many ways to see a problem, *amigo*,' said Velasquez. 'But justice, I think, should serve them all.'

The Don smiled, and nodded. 'We know you, *señor*. You are a man who seeks to do the right thing.'

The conversation ended and I excused myself to go. Out away from Rancho Pilar, the buckskin stepped out smartly, and I let him have his head. I wanted to study things out in my mind as we rode.

About ten minutes later, I realized someone was on my back trail. I lifted Buck into a lazy-looking lope that covered a lot more ground than a body'd think just watching him run.

The country kinda rolls between Saint Johns and Concho, and the hills are rounded and covered with grass and a few juniper trees. Once in a while, a cliff of malpais volcanic rock juts from the side of a hill. And sometimes those cliffs are split with cracks big enough to back a horse into.

I'd marked one of those cracks on my way in, and the hill was not more than a quarter of a mile away. The buckskin plunged around the edge of the cliff and stopped short at the touch of my knee. Seconds later, he'd backed into the crack out of sight. I piled off the horse and held my hand to his nose.

We waited, hardly breathing, for the rider on my back trail to make a play.

Soon the buckskin pricked his ears, but he wasn't nervous. That meant no Indian. He'd have been trembling all over if the rider had been an Apache.

At a suggestion of sound in the night, I gathered myself, raising my right foot to an outcropping. A horseshoe clinked in the night. A shadow came. I jumped, clapping my hand over the rider's mouth as I shouldered him off the horse. But the squeak that escaped my hand didn't come from a man. I was lying on top off a woman, my weight pinning her to the ground.

'Don't make a sound,' I growled, keeping my hand clamped over her mouth. She nodded, so I let go and stood up. She got to her feet, brushed the dust from her riding skirt, and tossed her head, sending a black cloud of hair swirling over her shoulders.

'You're as good as my people say you are,' she said.

I'd recognize that voice anywhere – I'd heard it in my sleep for nearly two years. 'Rita! You shouldn't follow a man around in the dark.'

'You are still on our rancho, Ness Havelock. I am quite safe here. My father's *vaqueros* are never far away. Would you like me to cry out and see how long it takes someone to come to my aid?' She moved out of reach. 'I find the one man with whom I would spend my entire life, Ness Havelock, and he rides away without so much as a word of explanation. Do you think I could let him ride away again without speaking?'

Astonished, I held my tongue.

'Garet told me you would return. He said I should believe in you. And now you have come back to step into danger. So be it. I know that is your way. But this time, do not ride away from me. *Por favor.*'

'Rita. I'm just a wandering half-Cherokee cowboy. I work for a dollar a day and found – when I can find a job. I got no right to court a girl like you. None.'

'I will decide whether or not you deserve me. Is that clear?'

I chuckled.

She turned serious. 'I wish to add my words to those of my father. This trouble has taxed him greatly. He is not as strong since he was wounded during the fight with Rafe Buchard's men. Now I fear for his life.'

'Why?'

'His heart is not strong. And he finds strange notes in unusual places around the hacienda. Threatening notes.'

'Do you have any of them?'

'No, Ness. He thinks no one else knows.'

'Rita, don't call me Ness. Ness Havelock is dead and buried in Moab, Utah. My name is Johnny.'

'I'm sorry. I thought—'

'Don't. Now, if you can get me one of those notes, it might help clear up this bag of wildcats. Can you?'

'But how can I find you?'

'Emilio Velasquez will know,' I said.

Standing so close, she smelled like a field of roses. I felt dizzy.

'Gracias.' She stood on tiptoes and kissed me on the mouth. The feather-light touch of her lips burned on mine long after she'd mounted her little paint horse. She gigged the pony down the hill and, as I watched, dark figures on horseback came from a stand of junipers to fall in on each side of her galloping horse. Don Fernando's *vaqueros* were on the job.

I turned the buckskin's head toward Silver Creek. I needed to talk to my brother.

CHAPTER 4

Rita Pilar's kiss burned on my lips far into the night. I had to figure out a way to defuse the powder keg in Saint Johns and all I could think about was her.

I shook my head to get rid of her, but she wouldn't go, so I surrendered and let the buckskin have his head. I wasn't fit for a woman like Rita, but I could dream. Maybe I even slept a little.

When we hit the wagon road to Show Low, I let the buckskin follow it while I thought about the tow-headed boy Harlow Wilson whipped to death in Mexican Hat. Don Fernando said other boys lived at Pitchfork headquarters, so I had to break up Wilson's game fast, or more boys might die.

Me and Buck hit Silver Creek in the gray of the dawn and turned north-west towards my brother's H-Cross horse ranch. About three miles from the house, the valley flattened out and Silver Creek widened and slowed, feeding meadowland on both sides of the stream.

Garet's house was solid – squared ponderosa logs with oak doors and shutters. Not a fancy place, but one large enough for a ranching family. It stood on high ground at the north-west end of the flats. Smoke from the chimney caught the first rays of the sun, and I heard a tin bucket clang and a calf bawled.

As I walked the buckskin into the front yard, I heard the click of a hammer being eared back. 'Just keep your hands on the saddle horn, stranger.'

I recognized the voice of Dan Travis, Garet's *segundo*. 'I'm friendly, Dan. Just let me take this hat off.'

'Do it slow and easy.'

I did.

'Ness!' Garet's voice came from the porch as Travis lowered his shotgun. I piled off the buckskin and met my big brother with a bear hug. Laura stood in the doorway and waited for us to finish our back-pounding and hollering.

'Look at you, Ness Havelock. You'd do for a scarecrow in our corn patch. A body would think you could dress proper when you come calling.' Laura's smile stretched the scars on her cheeks.

Then I noticed the little fist clutching her skirts. 'And who's that hiding behind you?' I asked.

Laura lifted the tyke and set him on her left hip. 'Meet your nephew, Beowulf Havelock.'

The boy stared at me from unblinking

yellow-hazel eyes. His shock of red hair matched his mother's.

'Shake, Beowulf.' I held out a finger, and the boy grabbed it with a fierce grip.

'Pleased t' meecha,' I said, moving my finger up and down. 'Cool little feller, ain't he?'

'Bo takes a while to get used to folks,' Laura said.

Garet's dog Brindle came sniffing at my boots, his tail wagging and I scratched him behind the ears. 'Looks like your killer dog grew up to be a house pet.'

Garet laughed. 'Him and Wolf are great partners.'

'Wolf?'

'Laura calls our son Bo. I call him Wolf. Doesn't seem to bother him one way or the other.' The boy reached his arms out to Garet, who took him and put him on the ground. Brindle sidled up to the child, offering a handhold of neck ruff to help him steady himself, and the two walked off, the toddler with uncertain steps and the dog patiently pacing the boy.

'I reckon they're off to watch the chickens,' Garet said, pride showing in his eyes.

'You must be famished, Ness. Come in. Breakfast is almost ready and the coffee's hot.' Laura stepped back into the house. Garet stayed outside to keep an eye on the boy.

'You know, Ness,' Laura said suddenly, 'you hurt Rita badly when you left.'

I nodded, not knowing what to say.

Bacon sizzled in a cast-iron skillet, mixing its smoky odor with that of hot biscuits. After forking the bacon onto a plate, Laura broke half a dozen eggs into the skillet.

'Chickens and milk cows,' she said. 'They make the difference between living and just getting by. Skunks keep trying to get into the coop, though. Garet traps at least one a week. The stink is awful, but it's better than losing hens and eggs.'

Laura rambled on while I sipped my coffee. She had her red hair clasped at the nape of her neck, but a few wisps hung wetly around her face as she worked at the stove. She poured gravy into a big boat and put it on the table, followed by a platter of biscuits and bacon. Places were set for four, and Laura added another for me. A high chair stood at the end of the table for young Beowulf.

Laura stepped to the back door and struck a hanging triangle with an iron bar. Minutes later, Garet, Dan Travis, and a young fellow I didn't know were seated with their faces and hands freshly washed. Beowulf banged on the table with his spoon. Laura gave Garet a look and bowed her head. The rest of us did the same. Garet said, 'Thank you, God, for the food we eat this day. Bless it for us, we pray. Amen.'

Laura smiled. Beowulf kept at his banging until Laura took the spoon and replaced it with half a buttered biscuit.

Garet introduced the new hand as Willy Bainbridge from New Mexico. He was a wiry lad who didn't say much, which spoke well for him in my book.

Breakfast went down good, and the extra cup of coffee afterward even better. The hands excused themselves and went back to their work. Laura cleared the table, and Beowulf smeared gravy in his hair.

'Well, Ness,' Garet said. 'What's on your mind?'

'You know Roland Prince? Well, he sent word through Isom Dart that he needed my help. And after that time in the Sonora desert, I couldn't say no.'

Garet said, 'Miguel talked about trouble at Rancho Pilar, too. I suggested he send for you. I've got a horse ranch to run, and besides, you're better'n me at sneaking around.' Garet grinned, stretching the zigzag knife scar across the left side of his face.

I told Garet and Laura everything that had happened from the time Isom brought word till I rode onto the H-Cross spread at Silver Creek.

We sat silent after I'd finished. Beowulf arched his back, wanting out of his chair. Laura wiped his hands and face with a wet cloth and turned him loose on the wooden floor.

'I got a feeling Harlow Wilson is behind a lot of this,' I said. ''Course there's Hanks's white-face cattle to reckon with, and his hiring Sid Lyle don't make things any simpler.'

'Don't know what to say, Ness,' Garet said. 'You know Prince. He's a straight shooter. And my opinion of Hanks is much the same. But things could be different now – something might be making them different.' Garet drilled me with a sharp look. 'And there's something else you'd better keep in mind. Ruel Gatlin's after your hide. Sooner or later, he'll find out you're not dead, and he'll come after you with his gun in his hand.'

He was right, blood feuds have a way of going way past reason, though I never thought to start a feud when I traded shots with those big Gatlin boys. 'Ruel Gatlin's not why Roland Prince asked me for help,' I said. I took a gulp of Laura's good coffee. 'Roland Prince is not the kind of man to give in without a fight. I saw him a couple of days ago and I have to admit he looked peaked. But he wouldn't let a shot in the back kill his spirit along with his legs.'

Garet said nothing. He'd wait until I figured things out my own way. He was like that, even when we were kids. He'd make me do it myself. Once he sent me out in the hills back of our house at Coody's Bluff in the Indian Nations when the Kansas Redlegs raided our place near the end of the war. Those renegades didn't find me, but their captain shot Garet in the knee. He made me help him take care of the wound and sent me after the Cherokee medicine man. Even though it was a glancing shot, it weakened that knee to where Garet has to wear a brace to keep it from buckling on him. But even with a bum knee, he's made his way as a lawman and now as a horse rancher.

'Something don't set just right,' I said.

'You gotta just keep working at it.' Garet fell silent for a moment. Then he fixed those black eyes of his on me and said, 'But once in a while you gotta shake the tree and see what falls out. If you ratchet up the tension on someone that's sneaking around trying to outsmart folks, they may trip up and make a mistake.'

I grinned at him. 'Shake the tree, eh?'

'When people try to get rich by breaking the law, they can only see how they want things to be. They figure nothing'll go wrong, and they keep thinking that way even when their careful plans are coming down around their ears.'

'Just you be careful, Ness,' Laura said from where she was wiping the dishes. 'A very good friend of mine is in love with you and she would hurt terribly if you were wounded or – God forbid – killed.'

Her talking about Rita was embarrassing. I knew well that I was just a shiftless rider and Rita was a landed lady. We were like black and white, me and Rita, and no amount of mixing would make either of us gray. While I loved Rita fiercely, I also knew I had to stay out of her life. But I wasn't going to argue the situation with Laura.

'I'll be careful,' I said. Laura gave me a sharp look. Sometimes a woman can see right through a man, no matter what he does.

'I know you want to get back to Saint Johns,' Garet said, 'but why not stay a day? Extra bunks in the bunkhouse, and you need a good night's sleep. Besides, I've got some young stock I think you'll be interested in. Appaloosa.'

So I turned off my Saint Johns problems and enjoyed the H-Cross ranch. Beowulf and me got acquainted and Brindle watched over the two of us as I fished for trout and Beowulf played in the mud of Silver Creek.

For supper, Laura had a pot roast of venison with new potatoes and green onions from her garden. Life at H-Cross was good. But the situation in Saint Johns kept intruding on my thoughts like storm clouds moving across a sunny sky. Yet despite my crowded mind, I went to sleep in the bunkhouse right after supper and didn't stir a muscle until daybreak.

Breakfast was flapjacks, butter, honey, and sausage, and plenty of it. No sooner had I finished than Emilio Velasquez rode in and brought me back to reality. He came with his hands shoulder high and a big grin on his face. 'Is this any way to greet a friend of your brother's?' he asked Garet. 'I am Emilio Velasquez from Ciudad Juarez, where we are quite fond of *Señor* Johnny.'

Garet gave me a raised eyebrow, then invited Emilio to get down and come in.

'*Gracias, señor. Con mucho gusto.*' Velasquez looped his horse's reins over the hitching rail and joined us for some of Laura's coffee.

'*Señora,*' he said gallantly. 'This coffee must have grown with direct blessings from God, or else it would not have been worthy of being brewed by such an angel as yourself.'

Laura giggled. Beowulf, still in his high chair, threw half a flapjack down the length of the table. Laura picked him up and hauled him into the other room, leaving the three of us at the table.

'As I said, *señor,*' Velasquez spoke to Garet, 'in Ciudad Juarez, your brother has more than once come to the aid of poor people who were at the mercy of tyrants.'

Velasquez tended to overstate things.

When Garet remained silent, Velasquez

fell silent, too.

'You're a long way from Rancho Pilar, *amigo*,' I said. 'Has something happened?'

Velasquez pulled a folded paper from the pocket of his short jacket. 'The *Señorita* de Pilar said I was to deliver this into your hands.' He held out the paper, which was charred on one edge. Words cut from a newspaper said:

DEATH TO YOU AND YOURS UNLESS YOU GO BACK TO MEXICO WHERE YOU BELONG. VENGEANCE IS OURS.

Someone wanted the Pilars off the land that had been their home for nearly a hundred years. And if the Pilars left, their land grant would go to whoever had the power to take it. In a flash, I understood. Whoever was leaving the notes would make an offer to buy Rancho Pilar, probably pennies on the dollar, but if the patriarch were running scared and determined to leave for Mexico, the offer might be accepted. Pennies on the dollar would be better than nothing.

Velasquez gave me one of his wide smiles. 'One more thing, *amigo*. People know you are here. It is no longer advantageous to dress like a peon.'

I turned to Garet. 'I don't know what all this is gonna mean to your spread, but the sign points to some greedy son who wants to profit a lot without rolling up his sleeves at all. Time to shake the tree.'

Garet nodded. 'Do what you think is right. But if you run into trouble, remember that I keep my guns cleaned and oiled.'

I knew that, but it felt good to hear him say it just the same.

Emilio stood watching Beowulf and Brindle when I led Buck into the front yard. 'This dog is very gentle. He watches young Wolf very carefully,' he said.

I laughed. 'Yeah, he's gentle all right. Wasn't two years ago that he tore out a man's throat.'

'I don't believe you.'

'It's true. Two years ago, a man attacked Garet's wife. That's where she got the scars on her face. Well, that gentle dog killed the man who did it. Yeah. He's some gentle dog. I'd hate to be anyone who tried to put a hand on that little boy. They'd have Brindle to deal with, and he's a lot of dog.'

Brindle, ignoring us, walked slowly beside Beowulf, again serving as a living handhold.

As we swung up, Laura came to the door with a bundle. 'Sourdough biscuits and bacon,' she said.

'Obliged,' I said and stuffed the bundle into my saddlebags.

'Ness. Here.' Garet flipped something at me. By reflex, I caught it with my left hand. I glanced down to see a double eagle in my palm. Trust my brother to know my last few cents were rattling a lonely tune in my pocket.

'Get some decent clothes,' Garet said. 'Pay me back when you can.'

'Thanks. I'll stop at Becker's store.'

'No need to go so far, *amigo*,' Velasquez said. 'Berado's in Concho will have everything you need.'

I nudged the buckskin down the trail, with Velasquez on his chestnut sorrel alongside. Garet and Laura watched until we dropped out of sight. The boy and the dog pursued their own adventures.

CHAPTER 5

We rode into Saint Johns with me looking like Ness Havelock again. I'd bought gray whipcord pants and shield-front shirt at Berado's, along with a good pair of black boots, black leather vest, and his only straight-brimmed, flatcrowned hat.

All the way from Concho to Saint Johns, I stewed over that dead boy. He'd been the kind of boy a man would feel good having grow up beside him. Damn that Wilson!

At the livery, I paid the hostler for the mule and the grulla mustang, and me and Emilio rode for the big house on the edge of town where Wilson set up Pitchfork head-quarters. Emilio led the mule and I the grulla.

A man on the screened porch saw us coming. He must have called a warning to someone, because another came out of the house with two rifles. He passed one to the first man and they both jacked shells into the chambers.

We stopped fifty feet out. Emilio had drifted off to my left a good twenty feet.

'I'm Ness Havelock,' I called out. One of the men was Ace Cruger, the other I didn't know. 'Howdy, Ace,' I said. 'Thought you worked for Prince.'

'He loaned me to Judge Wilson.'

'Whadda ya want?' the other man barked. He was stockier than Ace, shorter but wider through the shoulders.

'Who's your friend, Ace?' I asked.

'The Pitchfork boys call him Pecos. That's where he come from.'

Pecos scowled. 'State your business, Havelock, or I'll start talking with lead.'

I turned my gaze to Pecos. 'You don't want to try that, Pecos.' I held his eyes with mine until he looked away.

'I came to see Harlow Wilson,' I said to Ace Cruger.

'Boy!' Ace yelled.

A youngster about ten scuttled from the house and came to attention like an army private. 'Yessir, Mr Cruger!'

'Ness Havelock to see Judge Wilson, son. You run and tell him, OK?'

'Yessir, Mr Cruger. I'll go tell him.' The boy was off at a run, but I still noticed the thin scars on the backs of his arms.

We sat and waited. Ace and Pecos lowered the muzzles of their rifles a tad.

A door slammed inside the house. An angry voice came, along with a splat and a yelp from the boy. Heavy boots clomped toward the door, and Wilson stepped out on to the porch. A quirt dangled from his right wrist, and his blue eyes were wide with anger. The boy cringed in the shadow back of the door, a red welt on his cheek and neck.

Wilson didn't recognize me, but when he saw the grulla mustang, he took a closer look at my face.

'Look at me real good, Wilson. You'll remember last time we met outside Mexican Hat. That poor little tyke died without a name, but I'll tell you mine – Johannes Havelock. Most folks call me Ness.'

Wilson's eyes were defiant. 'I know of no one's death,' he said. 'The boy was very much alive when I left. If he died, who's to say it wasn't by your hand? I'd guess you're no stranger to killing. But I am proud to say, sir, that not a single human being has died under my hand.'

My anger turned me cold and hard as steel.

'Harlow Wilson, as I live, your whip took the life of that boy. And I see by the face of yonder youngster you like to beat on little ones.'

'Discipline is vital,' Wilson said. 'And as I am the legal guardian of every boy here – I don't receive a cent for their keep – it is my responsibility to see they grow up well disciplined and productive.' He slapped the quirt against his leg.

'Folks in Mexican Hat saw what you did

to the boy. I tried to patch him up, but I wasn't good enough. Be warned, Wilson. I'll be watching everything you do. Sometime you'll make a mistake, and I'll be there to make you pay for that young man's life.'

Velasquez spoke. 'And where my *amigo* Ness Havelock is not, I will be. Our eyes are upon you, killer. Our ears shall hear your every move, and our noses shall pick up the stench of your footsteps when there is no other trail to follow.' Emilio's eyes bored into Wilson's. I was glad to have him along.

I held the reins of the grulla out to Ace Cruger. 'Ace, you be real careful: you're in a sidewinder's den.'

Wilson slapped the quirt sharply against his leg. I sat the buckskin quietly, sensing that Velasquez kept an eye out for snipers. I focused on Wilson, the disgust I felt to the bottom of my soul written on my face.

Wilson smirked. 'How do you know a rifleman would not kill you if you so much as moved a finger in my direction?'

'Wilson, Zach Decker's the only man in these parts who can draw fast enough and shoot straight enough to beat me. I made myself clear at Mexican Hat: I'm only interested in you, Wilson. And no rifleman's fast enough to save you. Not one.'

My hands rested on my saddle horn, the accepted sign that I was peaceable. But my right hand was atop my left, and with it I could put a bullet through the third button on Wilson's fancy shirt before he could finish blinking.

I shifted my gaze to the boy who stood at attention beside the door. He kept his eyes on Harlow Wilson, tensed and coiled to jump into action should Wilson give him an order.

'What do you say, son?' I asked the boy. 'Do you want to stay here? You can ride away with me if you want.'

The child threw me a scared look. 'Oh, no, sir. Judge Wilson takes good care of us, from the goodness in his heart, he does.' The lad was buffaloed. Wilson smirked.

Damned if Wilson didn't think beating those boys was good for them. Damned if he didn't think the ecstasy he felt when whipping them came from doing the right thing. Damned if the man wasn't touched in the head. The most dangerous kind of killer.

'Remember what I said, Wilson.' My voice was hard as flint. 'And every time you see that grulla mustang, remember that boy in Mexican Hat. I buried him without a proper name, so you tell me what it was.'

Wilson's lips thinned out, and he said nothing for a long time. I sat on the buckskin and waited.

'Ronnie Dunne,' Wilson said at last. He spun on his heel and disappeared into the house, the youngster trailing along behind.

Ace just stood there, ill-at-ease and confused, holding the reins of the grulla in one hand and a rifle in the other.

'When next you see Roland Prince,' I said to Ace, 'you tell him I'll be around to see him directly.'

Cruger nodded.

'*Vamos, amigo,*' I said to Velasquez, and we rode away. Half an hour later, we were drinking mescal in the cantina. We hefted our second drinks before either of us said a word.

'Emilio,' I said finally, 'Harlow Wilson's got things stirred up around here, but any man who beats on kids and likes it has got to be twisted in other ways, too.'

Velasquez downed his drink in a gulp, sucking lime and licking salt from his knuckle.

'Folks from Texas are flooding this country, and you know what Texans think of Mexicans.'

He leaned back in his chair. 'Why punish Don Fernando for something done years ago and far away? What does he have to do with fights between *Tejanos* and *Mexicanos?*'

'Whoever's behind those death notes is trying to make Don Fernando afraid for his family and those who work for him. Look, all the old Mexican families have sold out to the gringos except for Don Fernando.'

'The Don, and especially *Señorita* Margarita, they think of themselves not as *Mexicanos* but as *Norte Americanos*. They have no place below the border to go.'

'I know. Don Fernando is the third generation at Rancho Pilar. That's a hundred years. But someone persistent might make him leave. And if the Pilars left, what do you think would happen then?'

Velasquez wrinkled his brow and worked the mescal glass round and round in his hand. 'Many people would no longer get wages and I think the town of Concho would die, though the mission would hold on a little longer.'

'If the Don decided to move his family to Mexico, he would need to sell his land for much less than it is worth,' I said. 'That, I think, is the real reason for the death notes.'

'Surely you are right,' he said. 'But what can we do?'

'Could I ask you to ride out to Rancho Pilar with a message?'

'*Seguramente*. But why not go yourself? The *señorita* would be happier to see Ness Havelock.' He gave me a sly smile, but I wasn't feeling playful.

'I'm going into Saint Johns to see Sheriff Hubbell,' I said. 'I've got to tell him what we'll be doing.'

Emilio nodded.

'One more thing: would you mind leading that razorback mule to Rancho Pilar? Just turn him out to graze. If we ever need a good pack animal, he'll do.'

'Of course. Does he have a name?'

'No one would ever give a name to an animal like that. Just call him Damn Mule, or Razorback, or whatever you will.'

Emilio laughed, but I was peeved because I'd had to ride that motherless creature all the way from Moab. OK, the mule was a tireless beast, but he was also the devil to ride.

I left the mescal glass half full. 'I'll get to see Hubbell before dark. You ride for Rancho Pilar whenever you're ready.' I clapped my gray Stetson on my head and automatically checked the action of my .44 Frontier Colt.

'Are you expecting trouble, *amigo?*'

'No. But I won't have time to check my weapon if trouble comes. It's like sleeping; you do it when you've got the time.'

I shoved the Colt back into its holster high on my left hip. I'd practiced drawing and firing that Colt so many times over the years that I no longer had to think about it. The gun just jumped into my hand and the bullet hit whatever I was looking at.

Velasquez rode away on his bright chestnut sorrel with its blazed face and three white stockings. By nightfall, he'd be under the same roof as Rita Pilar. I wanted to go with him, but couldn't.

Me and the buckskin ambled down the street and clopped our way across the log bridge into gentile Saint Johns. Jerry Simpson stood out front of the Longhorn, and his eyes widened when he saw me wearing my new gray duds. I raised a finger to him and kept Buck at a walk.

I rode past Solomon's Mercantile and the Higgins House. The sheriff's office sat cheek by jowl with the Saint Johns Advocate. A horse stood hip-shot out front so I tied Buck next to it, knocked on the door, and walked in.

The man with the five-pointed sheriff's badge on his vest had the bottom drawer of his desk pulled out for a footrest. His boots were in good condition but they'd been used. I could see where stirrups had rubbed against them.

'Afternoon, Sheriff. I'm Ness Havelock. Maybe you remember me bringing in Rafe Buchard about a year and a half, two years ago?'

'Thought I'd seen your face before. So what brings you to Saint Johns?'

'It's a long story,' I said. 'Mind if I sit down?'

He hooked a chair over with his foot. 'Help yourself.'

'I was north of Moab on the Trail when word got to me that Roland Prince needed help.'

64

Hubbell looked his question at me, and I told him the whole story. He pursed his lips under his iron-gray moustache. 'I knew Prince and Hanks had a falling out,' he said, 'but this looks like more than a spat between old saddle pals.'

'I promised Don Fernando I'd do what I could. And I owe Roland Prince.'

'So what do you want from me?'

'Well, sometimes you have to shake the tree to see what falls out,' I said, quoting Garet. 'I reckon I'll be doing a bit of shaking.'

Hubbell opened the center drawer of his big oak desk and pulled out a star. 'I'll deputize you if it'll help.' He held the badge out to me.

'Thanks, but sometimes it's better just to be someone helping friends. I appreciate the offer and if things come down to that, I'll be asking for the badge later.'

'Suit yourself, but you let me know whatever you find out, y'hear?'

'I'll do that. Sheriff, have you heard anything about Ruel Gatlin or J.T. Carr lately?'

'I got information on Gatlin. He shot a youngster over cards up in Wyoming, but the boy lived. J.T. Carr, he's the US marshal outa that state, ain't he? Haven't heard a word about him. Why?'

'I saw Carr in Moab; he was trailing Gatlin. Seems Gatlin bears me a grudge for defending myself against his brothers.'

The sheriff gave me a hard look. 'So you got Sid Lyle and his bunch gunning for you, and Ruel Gatlin's hankering to put daylight in your hide.' Hubbell chuckled. 'Not a very good recipe for old age.'

I put my hat on. 'I'm going over to the Claymore next. Maybe I can talk sense to Hanks and he'll pull Lyle off.'

Hubbell chuckled again. 'You're welcome to try. Me, I gotta collect taxes. You'd think, with all the hardcases around the county, the commissioners would let me sheriff a bit. But no. They want taxes gathered. Tax collector. That's me.'

'Don't think I'd want your job,' I said.

Hubbell turned serious. 'Ness, looks to me like there's some high stakes in whatever's going on. Whoever's the kingpin, they'll be more than happy to plug you in the back if they get a chance. Sure you don't want that badge? Some shy away from killing an officer of the law.'

'No. Maybe Ness Havelock, friend, will be less threatening to them.'

Hubbell dropped his feet from the desk drawer and stood up, a blocky man of average height. He stuck out a hand, and I was glad to shake it. At least the law wouldn't be on my back.

I paused a moment in the dusty street. A wagon had pulled up in front of Solomon's, and a bonneted woman sat in the seat while a man loaded supplies. The condition of the wagon and the team made me figure them as nesters, and the few supplies going into the wagon suggested they weren't doing too well.

I mounted Buck and rode past the wagon, tipping my hat to the woman, and reined in at the Higgins House. Might as well get a good night's sleep before going out to the Claymore.

CHAPTER 6

I woke from a dream with Rita's kiss burning on my lips and confusion in my heart, but I still had to go see Preston Hanks. After steak and eggs in the hotel dining-room, washed down with a couple of big cups of scalding coffee, I felt closer to being ready for the day.

Buck got his rest and plenty of oats over night, so he was ready to move out, and with his quick pace, we got to the Claymore Cattle Company just after noon.

I rode up to the front gate unchallenged, leaned down, slipped the leather off the post, and swung the gate wide enough to get Buck through. The click of a cocking hammer was nearly masked by the creak of the gate, but I heard it. The rifleman stood in the barn loft, where he could cover the whole front yard. I didn't let on.

A boot toe stuck out from behind the bunkhouse door, gunman number two — and there were probably more.

I scanned the grounds from under the brim of my gray Stetson. The buckskin walked up to the hitching rail and stopped. I hoisted my leg up over the saddle horn and dropped lightly to the ground. By that time, I'd located five men, one of them up on the ridge with a long gun.

'Hello the house,' I called.

A tall blond man with blue eyes and the supple hands of a fiddler stepped through the front door. His right eye showed a tiny tic.

'Hello, Sid,' I said.

'Lotsa folks know my name.'

'Tell Mr Hanks that Ness Havelock's here to see him.'

The gunman's gaze sharpened. 'Lotsa folks want to see him,' he said.

'Look, Lyle. You've got five men out there who are trying to keep their sights on me. But there's only one of you. Chances are you'd be dead before any of them could pull a trigger. Then where would you be? Wouldn't it be a good idea to invite me in to talk to Mr Hanks?' As I was talking, I plucked my Colt .44 from its holster and showed its business end to Lyle. He didn't like the fact I'd gotten the drop on him, but he simply turned and led me through the door.

Preston Hanks was in his study, a dark-paneled room with rows of leather-bound books on the shelves. The drapes were drawn and the place was almost dark as night. Preston Hanks sat with his head down on the desk, drunk. Men will drink, even in daytime. But Hanks was far gone. He sat

69

with both hands extended in front of him on the green felt of the desk blotter.

'Sorry to bother you, Mr Hanks.' Lyle's voice was polite, but carried a bit of scorn. 'Ness Havelock's here to talk with you.'

Hand trembling, Hanks waved toward the door. Lyle left.

I walked over to Hanks, Colt still in my hand, and backhanded him across the mouth. 'This country's about to blow up,' I said. 'You don't have the right to get drunk.'

The door crashed open and Sid Lyle barged in to find himself looking down the bore of my .44.

'No problem, Lyle. Why don't you see if you can get a gallon of the blackest coffee your cook can make?' I cocked the Colt.

He was back pronto with a big pot of coffee. He set it on the table and left me to work for the better part of two hours getting Preston Hanks sobered up enough to talk straight.

Strange. Here was Preston Hanks, one of the biggest ranchers in the country. A man who had cut a small fiefdom from the wilds of Arizona with his guts, work, and two bare hands. Yet he was blind drunk in a dark and musty room in the middle of the day. It didn't make sense.

Preston Hanks finally spoke. 'Whadda ya want?'

'I was riding the Trail, Mr Hanks, when a

man told me a war was shaping up in this country. He told me I oughta do something about it, and that's what I'm here trying to do.'

'War? Whadda ya mean, war? This here's peaceful country. All of it.' Hanks was eyeing the remains in the whiskey bottle with a hungry look. I opened a curtain and threw the bottle out the window.

'You got hired guns, and you say this is peaceful country?'

A wild look came into Hanks's eyes. 'It's them notes. Someone's gonna kill me. I find those damn notes all over. They're driving me crazy!'

'Anyone shot at you yet?'

'No. But they will.'

'Could be. But maybe the notes are meant to rile you up and shake your confidence. Do you have one of those notes handy?'

'I burn 'em. Nobody knows about them but me.'

'What do they say? When did you find the last one?'

'This morning, tucked under the skirt of my saddle. "The face of death is upon you", it said. "Your life is a blight upon this land. You die!" That's what it said.'

'Recognize the hand?'

'The words were cut outa the newspaper.'

Preston Hanks was getting threats, so was Don Fernando. Did Roland Prince get

71

notes, too?

'Hanks,' I said. 'I suspect you've been near cleaned out more than once, by Indians, or winter, or drought. Folks say you're a bad man to tangle with, even if you've English dudes for partners.'

'I only took on the Englishmen because I needed cash for Herefords.' Hanks's expression said he put store by those cows.

'Thing that bothers me, Hanks, is why you're letting the notes drive you around the bend. I wouldn't of figured you as that kind of *hombre.*'

Still, there was fear in his eyes.

'The whole thing sets wrong with me,' I said. 'Now I'm just a trail rider, but I like to see things set right. So if you'll keep your hired gunhands to home, I'll see if I can find out what's going on. Deal?'

Hanks nodded. He looked relieved. Maybe he'd stay away from the bottle, too.

'I'd like to talk to Lyle,' I said. 'Could you call him in?'

'Sid! Come on in here for a minute.'

Lyle came in – wary, drum-head tight.

'Lyle, I know you or one of your bunch shot me in Moab. Left me for dead. And Hanks, I figure you told him to do it. Felt you needed to protect your brand. I understand that.'

I looked Sid Lyle in the eye.

'I know you from El Paso, Sid. People

there say you ride for the brand. Nobody tops Sid Lyle when it comes to loyalty, they say. Now I've made a deal with Mr Hanks. I'm gonna find out who's trying to booger him. While I'm doing that I'd appreciate you keeping a sharp watch out around here.'

Lyle nodded.

'Nothing personal in Moab, Havelock,' he said. 'I reckon we can protect Mr Hanks. Do what you have to. And if you need help, holler. We'll come riding.' He grinned. 'I shoulda known Ness Havelock wasn't that easy to kill.' He stripped off this right glove and stuck his hand out. 'Mind if I shake your hand?'

I shook.

'You boys stand guard over the Claymore, Lyle. Counting on you.'

'We'll do it.'

Me and Buck headed back to Saint Johns, making town just in time for supper at the Higgins House. And on the way back, I realized I'd overlooked one of the best places for information – the newspaper.

Supper was roast venison, chopped new potatoes pan-fried with onions, hot gravy, and fresh baked bread. The meal took the edge off my hunger, but left plenty of room for a healthy slice of apple pie slathered with thick cream. Only Laura Havelock could put a better meal on the table. And the aroma from my cup of Arbuckle's best made the whole day take on a rose-colored tinge.

After putting up Buck in the livery stable, I wandered down Commerce Street to the little false-fronted building that housed the Saint Johns Advocate, William Sessions, Proprietor. A light burned inside, so I walked in. A bell over the door jingled and a spare man, tall and stringy, hands black from setting type, stood up from behind the counter.

'Howdy. Help you?'

'Like to see some back issues.'

'Help yourself. Pile of old papers there at your left, a year's worth, I'd guess. If you want to go back further, you'll have to go to the back room.'

'A year's probably enough,' I said. 'Thanks.'

He smiled and went back to setting type.

I turned up the lamp a mite and settled down for a long read. By midnight, I'd plowed through the fifty-two papers that covered the last year. There wasn't much there, but one article had me puzzled.

CATTLE MAGNATE COURTS SPAN-ISH GRANT HEIRESS

Judge Harlow Wilson, owner of the Pitchfork Ranch, was recently seen in the company of Señorita Margarita Pilar, daughter of Don Fernando Pilar, third generation owner of Rancho Pilar, which occupies the Santo

Domingo Pilar land grant of 1726.

Don Fernando's flocks number in excess of 10,000 sheep from which he harvests several tons of prime wool each year. Señorita Pilar is the only daughter of Don Fernando and is joint heir to the Rancho with her brother Miguel, as grants allow women to inherit as well as men.

Asked by this scribe as to his intentions concerning the señorita, Judge Wilson merely smiled and said his intentions should be plain for all to see and that he would let people make their own judgements. Señorita Pilar seemed slightly uncomfortable at all the attention, but we are sure she realized that Mexican women hardly ever venture into the part of town that lies east of the Little Colorado in Saint Johns. Nor did Judge Wilson seem to be disturbed by the impropriety of his being seen in the company of Señorita Pilar.

Señor Miguel Pilar, the señorita's older brother is away on business, she said, and Don Fernando was not available for comment.

This journal wonders if Judge Wilson does not see the possibility that marriage to Señorita Pilar would be the same as deeding half the Pilar grant into his hands.

What think you all, dear readers?

Rita had said she loved me, but I'd left without a word. She acted like she might still care for me when I saw her the other night, but who knows what a woman must do when politics get involved? I had no hold on Rita Pilar. Still, I was bothered to the pit of my stomach that a bastard like Harlow Wilson would be courting her. I didn't like it, but I could do nothing about it.

I thanked the newsman and left. Outside, I kept to the shadows, but still, he nearly got me.

CHAPTER 7

From the corner of my eye, I saw a slim man coming at me from across the street. 'Far enough, Havelock!' he barked, 'I'm Ruel Gatlin!'

He drew a gun as he shouted. I heard the click of his hammer coming back and I fell away. Still, his bullet took a big bite out of my left side. The Gatlins had shot me up before, and I knew I was hit bad now. But I couldn't stay put. Ruel Gatlin wanted me dead.

I struggled to my feet, pistol clutched in my right fist almost without thinking about it. Leaning against the wall of the alley I had fallen into, I waited for someone to show in the dim light of its mouth. Off to my left, weeds rustled against rough cloth. I switched my attention the other direction.

A red haze crept over my vision. The sound came again. The gun in my hand flamed of its own accord. In its flash, I saw a cowboy with his hands flung wide, falling as my bullet took him in the chest.

I dropped and rolled, groaning as I hit. The sound of my shot bounced off the wooden walls of the buildings that formed the alley. I found myself beneath a house, a good enough place to hide, except I was bleeding like a stuck pig. And that blood would show plainly where I was. I had to move.

I snaked along on my belly toward a far-off patch of light, never taking my eyes off it. Finally the hole was right in front of me. No one had come out to investigate the shots, but then, people seemed to be lying low in Saint Johns, and maybe Sheriff Hubbell was out of town collecting taxes.

I stuck my head out, stifling a moan that came with the stabbing pain in my middle. No Gatlin. I dragged my body out into the next alley, and rolled under the boardwalk. It hurt. Hurt like hell. Sweat poured down my face as blood oozed from the wound. Then footsteps sounded on the boardwalk. Not the random footsteps of a night-time stroller, but the careful steps of someone on the lookout. I held my breath.

Down the other way, another pair of footsteps sounded. Then a voice. 'Rolly's dead. That sumbitch Havelock shot 'im. But there ain't no sign of the bastard.'

'Lots of blood in the alley. Don't figure he's gone far. Take another turn between the buildings. He's likely holed up under one of 'em. Look for blood. He may be dead. I hit what I shoot at.' The voice was Ruel Gatlin's.

The footsteps went back the way they'd come. My brain wasn't working too well, but it told me I'd be dead if I went out on the street. Buck would have to stay in the livery stable.

As soon as the footsteps faded, I got myself out from under the boardwalk. Gatlin and the other gunman were checking all the alleys. They'd soon be back to this one.

Somehow I managed to stand up. My entire left side was half afire and half numb. Blood squished in my boot as I set out. But when I looked back, there was none on the ground. For the moment, my clothing and mud formed from blood and dust had stopped up the bullet hole.

Off to my left I heard the gunman call. 'Found his sign, Gatlin. He rolled under this house.'

In minutes, they'd find my trail out into the darkness. Got to get to the river. Why don't my muscles work?

'There's his tracks!'

Booted feet came on the run. A coal-oil lamp weaved and bobbed. I upped my pace, hunching along, I don't remember just how. I didn't even see the river, I just walked right into it. Right into water that felt like liquid ice, summer though it was. The shock of the cold water cleared my mind for a second. Sucking in a lungful of air, I managed to shove the Colt back into its holster and worked at keeping my head above water as the current swept me almost due north.

The cold numbed the wound, it numbed my fingers and toes, and it was working on numbing my mind when my hand struck something hard and round floating on the current. I clamped a hold on that little tree branch and pulled it up under my chin to where I could get my arms over it. No more than four or five inches thick and just buoyant enough to keep me afloat. But as the cold numbed me, it got tougher and tougher to keep my head clear and hang on.

A dog sniffed at my ear. I smelled the musk of sheep. A deep voice said something in Spanish. A tug came at my gunbelt, and my right hand flew up and grabbed whoever was trying to get my weapon. I opened my eyes to the frightened face of a Mexican man.

'*Por favor, Señor* Havelock,' he squeaked. 'I am Cesar Ramirez, *señor*. I herd the sheep for Rancho Pilar.'

I released my hold on his shirt and shut my eyes again. He gently removed the gunbelt and pulled out my shirt tail.

'You have bullet holes, *señor*,' Ramirez said. 'There is a small one in front and a larger one behind. I must take you away from here. The movement may be painful.'

I nodded.

Two people took my arms and dragged me away from the river. My side hurt like hell, and I felt blood start to flow from where Gatlin's bullet had exited. They loaded me into a wagon like a sack of flour, except flour don't leak blood. I heard a boy shouting commands to the dogs, who pushed the sheep onto the sandbar to eliminate the sign.

I don't know if I slept or passed out, but when I opened my eyes, the sky was dark. I lay on a piece of canvas against a ruined adobe wall. A campfire crackled nearby and the wall reflected its warmth. Half my body was covered with sticks. Another pile lay close at hand.

'Ah, *Señor* Havelock. I sent the boy Aldo for help. And as I cannot move you by myself, I will make you look like the packrat's home when I go to tend the sheep. If the one who shot you comes looking while I am away, he will see only the nest of a rat.'

'Water,' I croaked.

'But of course. A man always gets thirsty when he bleeds.' The shepherd brought a gourd full of water from the barrel strapped to the side of the wagon. I was almost too weak to hold the gourd while I guzzled at the water, but its coolness sent new life coursing through my tissues.

'*Gracias,* Cesar Ramirez. I owe you my life.'

'*De nada, señor*. My wife is second cousin to the wife of Pablo Baca. Your brother Garet returned poor Pablo's head so his widow and children could grieve him properly. You Havelocks have already given us more than we can repay.'

Ramirez fetched a gourd half full of hot broth. 'I forget myself. Here is a fine broth of sheep's knuckle, *señor*. It has much marrow from the bone. Old Mujer, the medicine woman, says bone marrow is good for those who lose blood.'

I sipped at the broth till the gourd was empty, then asked for more.

'Perhaps I should not tell you this, *señor*, but two men rode the river-bank today. First on the east side, then on the west. I think perhaps they search for you.'

'Then I should get out of here.'

'Oh no, *señor*. Not until the bullet holes have been cared for.'

'A man named Ruel Gatlin wants me dead. I can't worry about holes.'

'*Señor*, my wagon is the only way you can move. Wait, I beg of you. When Aldo returns, he will bring help.'

I didn't like the situation. Ruel Gatlin and that other man had searched for me in the river, probably all the way to the Colorado Bridge at Grant's Crossing and back again. Gatlin would remember the sheep camp and come looking.

'Just one more day,' Ramirez pleaded.

I finally nodded, but I figured I'd better do something about that bullet hole. I struggled out from under the rat's nest, using my elbows to pull myself along. Finally, I was sitting on the ground with my back against the adobe wall.

'Let's clean up these wounds,' I said. 'Boil me some water and get me a piece of cloth, *por favor.*'

While Ramirez was heating water, I took a look at the wound. The cloth over the entrance hole above my hipbone came away easily. The hole was small and round and puffy red and damned tender to the touch. It didn't look big enough for a .45 caliber bullet.

The cloth pad on the exit wound stuck to me. And I wasn't of a mind to force it. The bullet went in just above my hipbone and the blood-matted cloth on my back seemed to indicate it came out just below my short rib. I couldn't see the wound so Ramirez would have to clean it.

He came with a pot of hot water and a folded square of cloth that was once a flour sack.

'You got any more of that cloth?'

'*Sì*, an entire sack, *señor.*'

'OK. You're gonna have to help me.' I dipped the square of cloth in the steaming water and wrung it out a bit and used it to clean the entrance hole. The wound was mighty sore, so I took my time. I dipped the cloth again, wrung it out, and laid it on top of the wound until it cooled. The steam would help, I figured.

'Now, Ramirez, if you would use the hot water to loosen the cloth on the exit wound. Wet it down and leave it for a while. It'll come off.'

Easier said than done. That makeshift pad came off a lot harder than I'd figured. Ramirez worked at it for a long time, wetting and tugging and hurting, and it finally separated from my back, taking bits of pus and putrid flesh along with it.

'Wash the exit hole out, Ramirez. Make the water good and hot. I'll be OK.'

He tried to be gentle, but I felt like he was working on that hole in my back with a red-hot branding iron. By the time he finished, I was at the end of my string. I got him to smear two flour-sack pads with lard and tie them to me with strips from the sack.

With another gourd of Ramirez's broth inside me, I struggled back under the pack-rat nest and slept.

'Good morning, *señors*,' I heard Ramirez say. 'What might I do *para ustedes* this fine bright *mañana?*'

A male voice sounded, but I couldn't make out the words.

'Oh no, *señor. Aqui* is only two. *El muchacho*

Aldo goes to town *para café*. The herding of the sheep *es muy soledad. Me gusto el café, verdad?*'

Again the male voice. I opened my eyes to a solid crisscross of weathered gray sticks and stems. If I couldn't see out, they couldn't see in ... I hoped.

A horse walked between the adobe wall and the wagon. I could see its well-trimmed hoofs. The blacksmith had done a good job. Recent, too.

'We're looking for a man.' I recognized Ruel Gatlin's voice then. 'He's fairly tall, six feet or so, with black hair and eyes. Half Cherokee. He'd be wearing gray clothes and a black vest. Black boots, too. He may be wounded. He may be dead. You seen anything in the river, sheepman?'

'*Perdon, señor. Zee Ingles.* I am not so good. *Perdon.* Perhaps maybe, *el señor*, he speaks more slowly, no?'

Gatlin snorted. 'I'm not one for killing unarmed people, sheepherder, but you're stretching my patience mighty thin. Now. Have you seen anything in the river? Anything at all?'

'*En El Radito, señor?* The Little Colorado, as you say? No ... *pero momento.* Yesterday, early *en la mañana*, a large tree ... *uno* very dead tree with no leaves, it went down *el rio, señor*. It was *muy largo. Pero, esta todo.* That is all, *señor. Por favor.*'

Gatlin's horse stamped and blew. Another one answered from beyond the wagon.

'Mebbe we'd better have a look in the wagon, Gatlin,' another voice said.

The wagon! I'd been bleeding when they hauled me up here in that wagon. If that man found blood in the bed of the wagon, this rat's nest wouldn't hide a thing.

'Hey, greaser.' A saddle creaked as the other man dismounted. Ramirez's footsteps took him around to the far side of the wagon.

'Open 'er up, Mex,' the man said.

'*Si, señor.*' The tailgate dropped, rattling as it hit the end of the chains that held it parallel to the ground.

'*Mire, señor.* You see. Nothing.'

Metal struck wood. Rattles came from inside the wagon.

'They ain't nothing in here, Gatlin. I'll take care of the greaser, just in case.'

I heard the splat of a gun barrel striking a head, followed by a body crumpling to the ground.

'No need to kill him,' Gatlin said. 'Just a sheepherder. We ain't killers, Destain. We're looking for one. Havelock killed my brothers. And if he's not dead already, I'm gonna kill him. Come on. Let's go down the river again.'

'If he's floating, he'll go all the way to Woodruff, Gatlin. If he's sunk and snagged

86

along the bottom somewhere, we'll never find him.'

'I got a feeling, Destain. Ness Havelock's not dead. He walked to the river. He could have walked away from it.' The hoofs of Gatlin's horse moved away from my rat's nest.

'OK. One more turn down the river. If we don't find a body, we go back to Saint Johns and wait until he shows his face again. Shouldn't be too long.'

The horses loped away, but no sound came from Cesar Ramirez.

Silence. Damn. My gunshot wound was almighty sore. Damn. After a while a groan came from the other side of the wagon. Ramirez was alive.

I knocked some of the sticks away and saw the sheepherder's crumpled form on the ground near the wagon. I pushed at the heap of sticks on top of me, then dragged myself from under the nest with my elbows. The struggle took what seemed like hours, and it hurt. Bad.

Slowly, I pulled myself across the open ground where Gatlin's horse had stood a few minutes ago. At the front wheel, I grabbed the spokes and hauled myself to my feet. The flour sack binding held and the pads stayed on my bullet hole, front and back. Dizzy, I stood on shaking legs, panting against the pain. But I had to see to Ramirez. Getting

87

buffaloed with a pistol can do a lot more damage than just putting a man out.

I edged around the wagon with shuffling sideways steps, hanging on to the sides. When I reached the rear wheel, I stopped for a rest. That's when I realized I was barefoot. Where were my boots and socks? Apparently Gatlin hadn't seen 'em – and Destain hadn't found my gunbelt in the wagon.

Skirting the tailgate, I could see Ramirez, curled up with his head cradled on his folded arms. A bit of blood leaked from the split in his scalp where the gun barrel had landed. His straw hat lay some way away, probably knocked flying by the barrel of Destain's pistol.

The dizziness passed, and moving around the wagon added some strength to my legs. Maybe the old saying was right: a wound heals better when you stand on your own two feet.

Taking a deep breath, I went down on my knees beside Ramirez. I'd just put my hand on his shoulder when the click-click of someone earing back the hammer on a single-action pistol froze me in place.

'Well, well, Ness Havelock,' Ruel Gatlin said. 'I see you're not dead after all.'

CHAPTER 8

Ignoring Gatlin's gun, I mustered the energy to roll Cesar Ramirez on to his back. The sheepherder's eyelids fluttered.

'Cesar? *Amigo?*'

He groaned.

I heard Destain ear back the hammer of his weapon, and growl, 'Gatlin, what you waiting on? There he is. The man that killed Nick Rolly, and your brothers too.'

Holding my breath, I felt Cesar Ramirez's brow. Cool. His eyelids fluttered again.

'Cesar!' I shook his shoulder.

'Oooh, *Señor* Havelock. My head, it feels broken apart.'

Gatlin spoke. 'The sheepherder's not dead, Havelock. And I reckon it's time we had it out.'

Anger started building deep down inside. There I was, barefoot, shirt in tatters, belly wrapped with flour-sack strips, no hat, no gun, and Ruel Gatlin wanted a standup gunfight.

'All right, Gatlin.' I held my voice low, the words clipped short as they came out. 'All right. But take a good look first. Do you see a weapon? Can't you see I can barely stand,

89

much less pull a gun?' I didn't turn around. If I faced him, he might pull the trigger.

'Five years ago,' I said, 'they called me Johnny and sometimes that Havelock kid, because that's what I was and that's how I sometimes acted. I rode into Telluride from Ouray and your big brother Mort tried to run me off. I buffaloed him like Destain did to Cesar here. I had no quarrel with your brothers, Gatlin. I wanted to get some sleep 'cause I'd been in the saddle for two days and a night. But your three brothers came gunning for me. Just because I knocked Mort Gatlin down and didn't run.'

He seemed to be listening so I continued, 'Now, I don't know who fired the first shot, but when it was all over, your brothers were dead and I was bad shot up. You know what, Gatlin? When I rode out of Telluride trailing blood, folks cheered. That's what people in that town thought of your brothers. Now you've put lead into me. If you want to finish the job, you'd better get on with it. And you'd better shoot Cesar and Destain, too, 'cause they'll know you killed an unarmed man for no good reason.'

I'd said my piece. So I shut up and let him think about it. And I didn't turn, I just struggled to my feet, got some water from the water barrel on the side of the wagon, and knelt again to give it to Cesar. He gulped it, his eyes filled with fear. Then came the click of a hammer being released, and the rasp of metal on leather.

'Whatcha doing, Gatlin?' Destain sounded incredulous.

'I don't cheat. I don't kill unarmed men. Or cripples,' Gatlin said. 'Havelock, I'll leave you here with the sheepherder, and if you survive, we'll meet again. Then I'll kill you.' He wheeled his horse and cantered off toward Saint Johns. Destain followed.

I realized I was still holding my breath and let it out with a big whoosh. 'Come on, Cesar. You can get up now.'

Cesar struggled to sit. *'Ai yai yai.'* He cradled his face in his hands.

'Lie still,' I said.

Cesar collapsed to the ground.

I set out to make a pot of coffee, moving like the cripple I was. Dipping from the water barrel, I filled the pot, but barely managed to lift it to the fire and add the Arbuckles.

Cesar lay spread-eagled on the ground, snoring. Gatlin was gone, but I was a long way from being whole, and Cesar was anything but hardy. Still, we had to hang on until help came.

'*Señor* Havelock.' Cesar's voice was weak. With effort, I stood up from the wagon tongue and went over to him.

His eyes held a twinkle of mischief. 'Would that be the fragrance of *café* floating on the breeze, *mi amigo?* Might there be one cup left for a terribly wounded man who lies on the ground with his head in pieces?'

'Coming up, Cesar.' I chuckled, and it hurt. Back at the fire, I tipped the big pot to fill the cup rather than try to lift it.

When I returned with the coffee, Cesar was sitting up.

He sipped. *'Gracias a Dios por café,'* he said, and sipped again. *'Perfecto.'*

Cesar gave me a long look. *'Señor* Havelock, for the moment, your enemy has gone. But who knows when he will come again.'

I could only nod.

'Perhaps you should go to Rancho Pilar until your wounds heal.'

'I can't do that.'

'Por que?' His face was grave.

'My family is greatly indebted to Don Fernando. I cannot add to that burden.' Cesar could understand it in those terms, and I didn't have to mention Rita.

'Si, señor. Yo comprendo. But your wound is no scratch. You have one *muy largo* hole in your back. You need a place to get well.'

I had no retort. Gatlin had put holes in me all right, and the exit had yet to be stitched, and I didn't relish the thought.

We fell silent and passed the time sipping coffee. Our cups were nearly empty when we heard the jingle of harness and the rumble of wagon wheels.

Neither of us rose to meet the oncoming buckboard, but we kept an eye on it. Young Aldo rode one of the horses Cesar used to pull the sheep-camp wagon. He was bareback and his short legs stuck out from the big horse's sides.

'Aldo brings the *Señorita* de Pilar, *Señor* Havelock. And she comes with Old Mujer, who is a witch and a healer.'

That six-gun to the head had not damaged Cesar's eyesight. He'd probably recover just fine. Me? Well, Gatlin's bullet hole hurt so's I couldn't stand up if I wanted to.

'And why do you sit when ladies arrive?' Rita Pilar's voice carried an acerbic edge.

'*Por favor, Señorita* de Pilar,' Cesar said, then switched to English. '*Señor* Havelock has a grievous gunshot wound, and my own head has been broken in pieces with the barrel of a pistol. Standing is painful for the two of us, *señorita*, but we mean no offense.'

I read concern in Rita's eyes, and the graceful way she got down from the buckboard would have done an angel proud.

'*Abuela*, please see to *Señor* Ramirez,' Rita ordered. 'Ness Havelock, you come over here by the fire where it's warm.' She dragged the canvas pallet from under the rat's nest and brought it nearer the fire. I stayed put.

Rita threw me a sharp glance. 'Up, *señor*, and lie down here.'

'Don't think I can stand up,' I said.

93

'Try.'

'Can't.' I didn't have anything to grab hold of, and there was no way I could get up without help.

She came to stand before me with her long slim legs spread wide under her full skirt. She extended two hands. I grasped them. Lightning bolts ran up and down my frame as I touched her, but I held my face blank as she tugged me to my feet.

'Now, over there. Lie down.'

With her supporting me, I obeyed. I settled on the pallet near the fire where Old Mujer brewed something in a kettle.

'Over on your right side,' Rita said.

It hurt like blazes, but I turned.

She untied the binding and carefully put it to one side.

'The small hole is closing up nicely,' she said. But when she took the pad off the exit hole, her eyes tightened up. Something was not good.

'What is it?'

'Poisoning. Some flesh must be cut away or you will die. Old Mujer will do it.'

The old woman came over with a cup of tea. *'Tome,'* she said.

'It's willow-bark tea,' said Rita. 'It helps the pain.'

I drank it.

The old woman took a close look at the exit hole, clucking to herself and doing some poking. Somehow I kept from crying out.

'*Mescal,*' Old Mujer said to Rita, who got a bottle from Cesar.

The old woman started stropping a thin stiletto on a long strip of leather. She kept her eyes on me all the while, stopping now and again to test the edge by shaving some of the hair from her arm.

The medicine woman fired a long stream of Spanish at Rita, and beckoned Cesar and Aldo over from the fire.

'She says the cutting will be very painful,' Rita explained, holding out a stick about an inch thick. 'You are to bite on this. She will save your life, Ness.'

All I could do was nod.

The old woman told Cesar and the others to hold my arms, but I said, 'There's no need to hold me down, Rita.'

'But the pain...' Her voice had a catch in it.

'Give me something to get a grip on. I can take it.'

Cesar brought an old shovel handle from the wagon. 'Is this enough, *senor?*'

I gripped it. The old handle fit my hands fine. 'OK. Let's get on with it.' I put the stick in my mouth and grabbed hold of that shovel handle like it was salvation.

The old woman started slicing pieces off me. I grunted and groaned and chewed and tried to squeeze juice out of the shovel handle. She kept at it, once in a while having Rita dab the blood away with a piece of cotton cloth.

Now I'm no stranger to pain, having been shot more than once and tossed by unruly broncs a time or two. But the tip of that old woman's knife must have been white-hot from the fires of Hell. Sweat ran off my face and arms. She'd cut and I'd grunt and arch and she'd cluck at me and go after another chunk of bad meat.

When we got halfway to forever, Old Mujer poured mescal over the wound, cauterizing the whole crater of flesh – at least that's what it felt like. And she sewed me up with threads of sinew. Nor was she gentle about it. Once the hole was sewed up, she slathered the entire wound with gooey green cactus jelly.

'That is aloe,' Rita said softly. 'It makes burns and wounds heal cleanly.'

Only then I noticed Rita's hand on mine. I wondered how long it had been there.

'*Finito*,' the old woman said, and left the bandaging to Rita.

Torture takes a lot out of a man, and by the time the old woman finished with her knife, needle, and other instruments, I was all in. I lay face down on the canvas pallet and tried to breathe shallow so the bored-out hole in my back wouldn't hurt so damned much.

'You must get up, Ness,' Rita said.

I ignored her.

'Ness.' She put a hand on my bare shoulder that sent tingling ripples through my body. I grunted.

'Ness. Get up. Now is not the time for sleeping. You can do that later. Now you must get on the buckboard so we can get you away from here.'

'Leave me lie.'

'Ness Havelock, you must come. You must be where *Abuela* can care for you. You must.'

'Can't.'

'*Madre de Dios*, but you are a stubborn man. Must I strike you across the brow with a pistol and carry you away like a prisoner?'

I mustered up all the strength I had. 'Rita Pilar, get this through your head. Ruel Gatlin shot me. He's sworn to kill, but his warped sense of chivalry won't let him do it while I'm wounded and unarmed. But who knows how long he'll keep thinking that way?

'I think you want to take me to Rancho Pilar. But considering the notes your father gets and the threat of death I live under, that's not a good idea. Do you hear me?'

'No. What are you saying?'

'I can't go to the Rancho. I've got to stay out of sight, completely, until I can face Ruel Gatlin square, and if needs be, Baldy

97

Fontelle and that hot-tempered Destain.'

I couldn't see Rita's face, but a drop of something warm and wet fell on my back. Making her cry hurt me nearly as much as Old Mujer's stiletto, but I could see no other way.

'Cesar, tell me. Where can I keep out of sight for a few days?'

'Maybe two places, *señor*. One is the abandoned village of El Tule. It is only crumbled adobe now. The other is a cave. The cavern is further away, but I think the gunmen do not know of it.'

'I'll go to the village tonight. Have the dogs drive sheep over our tracks in the morning.' Still lying on my stomach, favoring the left side. I turned to look at Rita. 'I'm sorry, but you'll have to stay in camp until Cesar gets back.'

Reluctantly she nodded as tears welled from her dark eyes and rolled down her perfect cheeks.

I had half a day to rest and drink a lot more of Cesar's sheep-knuckle broth. By evening, he even had me chewing on some mutton, and it tasted mighty good. So when the time came to leave, I got to my feet on my own, with the help of the shovel handle. I had my ragged shirt on, and Cesar had washed the blood from my socks so I could put on my boots, too.

Rita arranged the canvas pallet on the bed

of the buckboard and added two Navajo blankets. A box of supplies went under the seat.

Leaning on the shovel handle, I shuffled to the buckboard. The pallet lay at the edge of the wagon bed. I lay down on it face down, and Cesar pulled me into the center of the buckboard.

Rita lifted her skirts and made to climb aboard.

'Stay here,' I ordered.

'How can I sit here all night wondering if you are safe?'

'You must. Right now, I don't want anyone to know where I go. What you don't know, you can't tell.'

'Ness! I would rather die than tell where you are.'

'I'm sure you think that. But don't come. Please.'

At last, Rita went back to the fire. I hated to leave her there, but what else could I do?

The sheepherder clucked at the team, and we started for El Tule at a walk. But even then, the buckboard jolted. With each jolt, I moaned and fought the waves of pain in my back. After a while, I told Cesar to take me to the cave – that might throw my enemies off for a while.

Without a word, he slapped the reins on the backs of the horses, and we jolted away in a different direction. Sometime after midnight, the buckboard stopped.

'From here we must walk, *señor*,' Cesar said, concern in his voice. 'Can you do it?'

'I'll do what I have to do. Shift me around so my feet drop off the buckboard.'

Cesar set the brake and came around to pull the pallet out over the edge. When my feet touched the ground, I bent at the waist, then used the buckboard bed to hoist myself to my feet.

In the moonlight, I could make out one of the cinder knolls that dotted the country. But this one had a malpais cliff on one side that looked as if a giant cleaver had chopped a slice from the hill and scattered cinders down the slope.

'Let's go,' I said, picking up the shovel handle. Cesar led and I stumbled along behind him with the handle acting as a third leg. He picked the best path he could, but I kept kicking cinder rocks, and every time I did, pain ravaged the hole in my back. I sweated, though the night was cool, and gasped for breath. It was the longest, toughest walk I've ever made.

'*Señor?*' Cesar whispered. 'I do not know if the cave is *occupado*.'

I could make out the darker opening in the malpais wall of the cliff. A big cinder boulder partially blocked the cave's mouth.

'Step in, Cesar. The smell will tell you if there's any kind of varmint in there.'

He hesitated, then bent down and entered. He was back in a moment. 'Only the smell of mice,' he said.

'Then build a fire a ways back from the mouth. That'll give us light.'

The fire was soon kindled and Cesar brought the pallet, the blankets, the box of provisions, two canteens of water, and a bundle of firewood. His final trip back to the wagon produced an old Spencer .56-50 rifle and my gunbelt.

'I have only a few bullets for the long gun,' Cesar said, holding out a cloth bag.

'Thanks.' I took the bag. It held no more than a dozen cartridges.

Cesar stood at the mouth of the cave.

'Come back in five days,' I said. 'And ask the *señorita* to lend me a horse. *Bueno?*'

'*Bueno.*' Cesar disappeared into the night. Soon the sound of the buckboard faded and I was alone.

CHAPTER 9

The riders came the second day. I'd scouted me a hold-out place in a gully north-east of the cave. And I had a spot in the shadows where I could watch a swathe of land that ran from Grant's crossing all the way past the Blues to the divide the other side of Round Valley. Beyond the divide, I could see Old Baldy, Mount Ord, and Wolf Mountain.

I caught the riders' dust over towards the Little Colorado just after noon. Those five could have been anyone, but I had a feeling they were Pitchfork men, because they came in a beeline for Twelve-Mile Knoll, which told me Cesar Ramirez had talked.

The Spencer and my Frontier Colt smelled slightly of the bacon grease I'd used to clean them. I had twenty-six bullets between me and Hell, and nine of them were rifle cartridges that looked as old as petrified wood.

I walked all hunched over like an old crone, but I got the old Spencer and a canteen of water from the cave, took them up to the gully, and forted up.

The five riders came right on, but I was not about to waste ammunition on long shots. They stopped at the foot of the knoll, and the big man lifted his hat and wiped his bald pate with a red bandanna. Baldy Fontelle. And I recognized the skinny jug-eared ranny from Mexican Hat called Petersen. Rod Destain was there, along with two more riders I'd seen but couldn't put a name to.

The Pitchfork men fanned out and started up the long incline from the foot of the knoll. I needed to get those riders afoot. I drew aim with that old Spencer, not knowing if the sights were off, and shot Baldy Fontelle's horse. I aimed for the torso right behind the front legs, but the bullet caught the big horse in the neck. The old gun shot high and to the right.

Fontelle kicked his feet from the stirrups and, Winchester carbine in hand, stepped off his mount as it went over on its side. The dying horse slid down the hill, legs kicking. Fontelle ducked behind a boulder.

A cloud of black-powder smoke marked my position, but I was out of sight. I ejected the spent cartridge from the Spencer and shoved another into the chamber. Damn single-shot shooting.

When I looked over the sights of the old gun for another horse, the four riders were scrambling back down the slope. Let 'em go.

'Havelock,' Fontelle's voice rang out.

'I hear you.'

'There's five of us and only one of you. I'd say you'd better give up. It's a done fight.'

'I got plenty of shells, Fontelle, and I hit where I aim. You want me, you come and get me. If you think you can.'

The answer was a puff of smoke and the whine of lead ricocheting from a head-shaped rock over to the right. I held my fire. I had them all spotted except for skinny jug-eared Petersen.

One of the riders left a booted foot out where I could see it. I adjusted my aim for the old rifle peculiarities. The old Spencer bucked as I squeezed the shot away, and boot leather flew as the ranny screamed. One down. Two bullets gone. Twenty-four left – but only seven cartridges for the Spencer. The long-range war couldn't go on much longer.

Three rifles answered my shot, sending lead whining off the rocks that protected me and showering me with bits of malpais.

'You're gonna have to shoot better'n that, Fontelle,' I taunted them. Sometimes an angry man will make mistakes.

'We'll git you, Havelock, before the sun goes down,' Fontelle shouted. 'You mark my words.'

The man I shot in the foot called out, 'Baldy, I'm bleeding bad,' he rasped, panic in his voice.

'Destain, crawl over there and take look at

Smith's foot,' Fontelle ordered.

I could see Destain crabbing over to Smith's position, but I didn't shoot him.

'He caught a slug in the ankle, Baldy. No way he's gonna walk nowhere,' Destain reported.

'Goddamn you, Havelock,' Fontelle shouted. 'You ruined a good man's foot.'

'If I read you right, Fontelle, you want to do a lot more to me than shoot me through the foot. Ruel Gatlin got lead into me three days ago, but I ain't nowhere near dead. You want to take that man to Doc Wolford in Show Low, maybe he won't die.'

Destain wasn't helping Smith at all. Finally he turned towards Fontelle. 'Baldy. I don't know what to do with this. Smith's bleeding bad.'

'Go take care of him, Fontelle,' I called to him. 'I won't shoot.'

Fontelle stood up, hands high. 'Truce,' he yelled.

'You got ten minutes,' I said. 'After that, bets are off.'

Fontelle walked over to Smith's rock and he and Destain pulled the wounded man out and laid him flat. Fontelle cut the remains of the boot from the mangled foot, disregarding Smith's yelps of pain. He collected four bandannas including his own and one from the rider who'd taken refuge behind a malpais upcropping. He folded two into thick pads and tied them over the wound with another. Then he rolled up the remaining bandanna and tied it above Smith's knee, slipping a foot-long stick under it and twisting it snug.

'Here,' he said to Smith. 'You hold on to this stick. The bandanna stops the blood, but you'll want to loosen it when your foot goes to sleep. Up to you. We've got to get Havelock.'

I used the truce to change my position, moving gingerly to a spot a dozen feet away.

Fontelle left Smith whimpering and hanging on to that stick for dear life.

'Come on, Destain, Pecos. We got a job to do.' Fontelle grabbed his rifle and sprinted up the hill. I had no chance for a shot and I wasn't going to waste bullets.

Suddenly, he stood up and took another run, firing as he came. He was down and rolling behind a low juniper before I could shoot, and I wouldn't pull the trigger without a good target.

Following Fontelle's example, Destain and Pecos scrambled in to cover closer to me. I needed to slow those rannies down or else they'd be all over me. The rock Pecos hid behind gave me the best line of fire. Fontelle rushed forward but I didn't shoot. Then Destain. It was Pecos's turn. The moment he stood up, I squeezed the old Spencer's trigger and lead dusted Pecos front and back. He crumpled without a sound.

My shot drew fire from both Fontelle and Destain. But I'd slid down the bank of the gully, dragging my canteen and the Spencer rifle. I only went ten yards, but the change of position was enough. I held quiet. Grama grass grew at the edge of the gully and boulders were strewn all around. I had no hat since I'd lost my new gray Stetson when Gatlin shot me.

I peeked over the edge. No one in sight. I reloaded the Spencer, then wiggled upward, taking care not to disturb the grass.

Fontelle rushed to a different cover. He wasn't more than fifty yards away. Then Destain moved.

For a time, things went dead quiet. A hawk screamed from his circle high above the knoll. A covey of quail broke cover up the hill a ways. They scurried down the east side of the gully. Then boot leather scrunched on cinders. Petersen was no woodsman. I took cover behind a boulder centered in the gully so I could see both banks. Petersen crunched more gravel.

I hoped he, Fontelle, and Destain didn't top out all at the same time. Then I saw Petersen's hat, but I couldn't tell if there was a head in it.

All three Pitchfork men were higher up the hill than me. I was shooting up, a disadvantage, but now I was closer to their horses than they were. Maybe I could sneak down the gully and get to those cayuses without Fontelle and them shooting me into doll rags.

The hat was a decoy. I could see Petersen peering around a big malpais, trying to spot me. Given the inaccuracy of the Spencer, it was a risky shot. Not much of him showed, but his cover downhill of the malpais was scrub brush. I had to narrow the odds.

I aimed at the mound of dirt below Petersen's searching eyes. His body was hidden by the bush. I touched off the Spencer and Petersen yowled.

'Petersen? He get you?'

'My God!' Petersen's voice held an edge of hysteria. 'He shot my ass off.'

I slid down the gully toward the horses.

'I'm bleeding. Baldy,' Petersen screeched. 'Baldy?'

'You hang in there, Pete. We got him in this gully. He can't go far with that gunshot wound Gatlin gave him.'

But I was already twenty yards away and moving as fast as I could without making noise.

'Baldy. I'm hit bad. Help me.'

'Just a few more minutes, Pete. We got 'im in here.'

Fifty yards away I got, and the gully flattened out. I stood up and started walking, stepping careful and wondering when they'd look back over their shoulders.

Petersen moaned over on the other side of the gully, and that tended to keep Fontelle and Destain focused that way.

'Destain?'

'Yeah.' The Pitchfork rider's answer came from higher up the knoll. I stopped, so movement wouldn't attract their eyes.

'You get over there and see what you can do for Pete,' Fontelle said. 'Ain't much of anywhere Havelock can go.'

I could see Fontelle snaking toward the bank of the gully. Wouldn't be long till he'd see I wasn't there.

'He ain't gonna die. Let's leave him be,' Destain said.

Petersen kept up his lament.

'Destain. I ain't gonna tell you again.'

'Havelock'll have a clear shot at me when I cross. I ain't ready to die.'

Destain figured I hit what I shot at.

'Good God! Just do it, will you? You been in fights enough to know how to keep to cover. Now move!'

Destain didn't answer. But I heard scrambling high on the hill going away. I started toward those four horses again, stretching my stride as much as I could with a bullet hole in me.

Smith's eyes were closed and he breathed fast and shallow. He smelled of blood and shit.

'Smith,' I said in a low voice. His eyes flew open. 'Don't make a sound or you're dead meat. I'm taking your horses, but I'll send help back. A man shouldn't have to die out here.'

He nodded and licked his lips. His right hand had a death grip on the stick that kept his life from bleeding away.

'Don't forget to loosen that bandanna now and again,' I said. 'Else you'll lose that leg.' I left him there.

The horses were ground tied a dozen yards away or so. I shifted the Spencer to my left hand, held out my right, and walked directly toward the sock-footed bay that stood closest. He stayed where he was. I gathered his reins and turned him so he stood between me and the hillside. I could still hear Petersen's cries, and I caught a glimpse of Destain as he crossed the gully. Fontelle was out of sight.

I stepped around the bay and shoved the Spencer into the saddle scabbard and looped the canteen over the horn and lariat. Biting my lip against the pain, I tried to raise my left foot to the stirrup. Wouldn't go that high. I almost echoed Petersen's moan. Had to keep trying. Again. Didn't make it. But the foot was going higher each time.

'Havelock!' A shot followed on the heels of Fontelle's shout, but it was wide.

This time, I got a foot in the stirrup and

hauled myself aboard that cayuse with the strength of my arms. I felt a stab of pain in my back and felt the wound tear. No doubt it'd bleed.

Fontelle took another shot that spanged away after smashing into the malpais. I slammed my boot heels into the bay's sides and loped him straight at the other three horses. They broke and ran, trailing the reins with their heads held high.

Fontelle came bounding down the hill, trying to get close enough for a good shot with his saddle carbine. I lugged out my .44 and slung lead at him. The bullet hit ten feet in front of him, but he ducked for cover. I reined the bay gelding around and we high-tailed it.

The bay jumped and came down running, but favored his left hind leg. The report of Fontelle's rifle followed. A slug had hit the horse. He limped, but I could only ride him as far as he could go. Then, if Fontelle caught up, we'd have it out.

I lined out for Concho, south and a little west, for it was the closest town and Rancho Pilar was only a couple of miles further on.

With Twelve-Mile Knoll more than a mile away, I slowed the gelding to a fast walk. We were a matched pair – him with a bullet in the hip, and me bleeding again from that exit wound. I felt sticky wetness begin to collect at my belt line.

I glanced at the sun. Late afternoon. If I was lucky and the bay held out, I'd be at Rancho Pilar by midnight.

CHAPTER 10

The night had hardly darkened when the sock-footed bay's limp got worse, but I was in no condition to walk. I decided to stay on the gelding as far as he'd carry me, even if he went slow. The chances of Baldy Fontelle coming after me in the dark were slim, him with two wounded men to look after.

I'd stopped bleeding, but the exit wound in my back was almighty sore. Four days going on five since Gatlin shot me, and I wasn't a whole lot better. Nothing to do, though, but grit my teeth and keep going. It wasn't in me to quit.

I let the bay set the pace, and I must say that pony had heart – he just kept plodding on, his head bobbing, favoring his left hind leg.

At midnight, we were still a long way from Rancho Pilar. The moon was out and the stars glittered, hanging so close a man could likely touch one with a long pole. The dusty scent of juniper wafted on the southerly breeze. The night would have been right fine for a cross-country ride if it weren't for the bullet holes in man and horse.

Baldy and Destain hadn't ridden up on

me yet; maybe they weren't coming. I'm a hard man, but not hard enough to ride away from two wounded men. Who could tell about Baldy Fontelle? And who knew how fast they could catch those loose horses?

Then the bay stopped. I clucked at him, urging him on with a boot to the ribs, but he paid me no mind. He stood head down and hipshot, taking the weight off his left hind leg.

I heaved myself up so I was standing in the stirrups, and swung my right leg over the cantle. The bay staggered and seemed about to go down, so I slid off. When I hit the ground, the jolt sent a lightning bolt through the wound, but the pain soon lapsed. Maybe I could walk after all. But then, why not sit down there and wait? By morning, the bay would be rested, and maybe I could ride again.

So I pulled the saddle off, slipped the bit from the bay's mouth so he could crop at grama grass, and hobbled him with the reins. In the blue light from the moon, a black line of blood showed from the bullet hole to his hocks, but it no longer flowed. We'd just have to see how sore he was come morning.

I found biscuits and bacon in the saddlebags, along with a packet of lucifers. But I couldn't make a fire. Instead, I used my clasp knife to shave off pieces of bacon and chomped them with cold biscuits, washed down with water from my canteen. The biscuits tasted so good I had three, not worrying about what I'd eat the next day.

Stomach full, I spread out the saddle blanket and, using the saddle for a pillow, laid down on my right side, closed my eyes, and waited for sleep. But instead of slumber, images of Rita Pilar filled my mind. I saw perfect portraits of her dark eyes and ivory skin, her white teeth flashing in a saucy laugh, her dark hair piled high on her head. And my ears strained to catch the lilt of Spanish in her speech.

A drifter and sometime cowboy with hardly two centavos to rub together, I had nothing to offer her. But she wouldn't let me sleep. Finally, the dawn brought light to the eastern sky. Nevertheless, the rest had done me good, and I got to my feet a bit easier. The bay stood almost as I had left him; likely he'd not be much good on the trail.

The land seemed almost flat, with Twelve-Mile Knoll blue in the distance. A rise to the east would give me a place to take a look over the back trail so I picked up the Spencer and checked the extra shells in my pocket, then made for the hillock.

When I first looked at my back trail, I saw nothing moving. I took time to survey the country, but I almost missed it. Then, from the corner of my eye, I noticed a line that didn't match the rounds and curves of the trees and rocks. I stared off to one side, purposely shifting my focus. There. A weathered roof line. A shack of some kind.

When I took one more look at the back trail, there they were. Two riders, Fontelle and Destain, no doubt, coming this way with heads down, watching the trail. They were still too far off to see me, but they'd soon be close enough. I limped over to the horse and threw the saddle on him. In daylight, his wound didn't look bad.

Rifle in one hand and reins in the other, I struck out for the shack, or whatever it might be. The horse came along, favoring his hind leg. I walked as fast as I could, and the horse kept up. Closer, I saw an abandoned log cabin with a lean-to. Its thick pine logs would give me a place to make a stand against Baldy Fontelle and Rod Destain.

At the cabin, I found an old corral, broken down and useless, but overgrown with a thick stand of pigweed – good feed for a hungry horse. I led the bay into the weeds and took off his saddle and bridle. I knotted the lariat from the saddle around his neck with a bowline and secured the other end to a solid old post.

For some reason, Harlow Wilson wanted me dead. I could understand Ruel Gatlin shooting me; I'd shot his brothers. But all

116

Harlow Wilson had against me was that affair outside of Mexican Hat and my nosing into whatever was going on in Saint Johns. To me, that meant he must be playing for mighty big stakes.

I left the saddle on the ground and went to inspect the cabin. Fontelle and Destain would ride up soon, and I had to be as ready as twenty-two cartridges could make me.

The little cabin was about ten by twelve inside, but carefully made. I wondered who dragged those pine logs to this lonely place. Maybe the cabin was someone's place to hide, being far from any town or well-used trail.

Inside, I had to clear away debris from the fallen-in roof to make standing room near the high window in the north wall. The door had fallen off and its framed opening gaped. I'd just have to avoid it. A smaller door in the south wall formed an escape route. I figured Fontelle and Destain would come riding straight in, and they did.

I decided to keep them off with the pistol, saving the few bullets of the Spencer for good shots. I knew the rifle now, and I reckoned I could hit what I aimed at with the old gun, but I wasn't about to shoot any man from ambush.

The cabin overlooked a good field of fire. Not a man-sized rock within a hundred yards, and all the junipers were small, new growth. I had rifle, pistol, canteen, and some cold biscuits from the saddle-bags, and I found a stool in a corner and decided to sit down and watch through the door. The sun shone through the pole rafters and warmed my back. Felt good on the bullet wound Ruel Gatlin put in me. A blue jay flitted down to strut in front of the door, cocking an eye in my direction.

'You strut around out there and you're likely to get your tail shot off,' I said to the bird. He ignored me.

In the hot sun, the temperature inside the old cabin soared. I sipped at the canteen, and I caught a whiff of the wintergreen scent of pine pitch. My eyes followed the lines of the logs, and found a big knot had bled pitch in the heat.

I took a look out the door. Fontelle and Destain were nowhere in sight. I picked up a stick and scraped up some of the pitch, ending up with a pigeon-egg-sized glob. Now, maybe I could keep that bay horse from getting flyblown.

The warped south door opened enough to let me out with the Spencer in one hand and the pitchy stick in the other. The bay horse cropped at the pigweed. I stood the Spencer against a post, patted the bay on the neck, and worked my way around to his gunshot hindquarter. I rubbed warm pitch all over the bullet hole. The bay backed away, but I got him gummed up with about three swipes. I threw the stick away and slipped back into the cabin.

When I looked out the north door, Fontelle and Destain had topped the rise and stopped their horses. Then they moved back to where I couldn't see them. Were they planning to sneak around back?

Half an hour or so passed without Wilson's men showing. I stepped across the jumbled sticks on the floor to peer out the back door. No riders. I went back to my stool. The field of fire was empty. Nothing stirred but grama grass tassels waving in the slight breeze. The sun beat hot against my back, and me without a hat. The back of my neck would be burned before sundown.

Had Fontelle gone back to his wounded men? Did he plan ambush for me further along the trail? One thing seemed certain: Harlow Wilson wanted me dead because I was nosing into the odoriferous goings on in Saint Johns.

What about the Pitchfork outfit? A ranch with no range, a headquarters with no cowboys. Just where did Wilson expect to run 50,000 cows? The Hashknife outfit owned a good part of the railroad land, and the Pilar Grant covered 100,000 acres between the Blues and Saint Johns. Smaller outfits like the Forty-Four, the Claymore, and the RP Connected took what there was left, so it looked to me like the Pitchfork had no range.

Clouds piled high above the Blues and began their march north across the skies like ranks of cotton balls in close-order drill.

Fontelle didn't show. But him and Destain might be hunkered down beyond the rise, keeping an eye on this shack and waiting for me to make a target. Maybe I ought to make them show their hand.

I stood up in the doorway, slowly counting to ten before stepping behind the wall. No rifle shot came. I searched the rise for anything that looked like a head. Nothing.

Stepping out the door, I walked around the cabin to check on the horse again. As I came back around the corner, a bullet thunked into the log siding followed by the bark of a rifle. Too long for Fontelle's short saddle carbine, and he wasn't all that good a shot anyway.

I ducked back into the cabin before the second shot came. I poked my head up at the high window, but couldn't make out where Fontelle lay. Although gunsmoke drifted off to the west, I wouldn't waste rifle cartridges shooting at something I couldn't see well.

With no field-glasses to search the line of the rise, I could only tempt Fontelle to shoot and hope I could get lead into him before he got me. The smoke had come from a lone scrubby juniper. Fontelle might be hiding there, and he might not. I pulled my Colt, stepped to the door, and snapped off three quick shots at the juniper.

Emilio Velasquez was nearly to Twelve-Mile Knoll when the sound of three shots floated in on the breeze. They came from the south. Velasquez reined his sorrel stallion in the direction of the shots. He put the big horse into a canter and soon came across the trail of a single, limping horse, followed by two shod mounts. Only two-to-one odds, he thought. Which means Ness will come out ahead.

He galloped the sorrel along the trail, his rifle held across the bows of his silver-encrusted saddle. When another shot sounded about half a mile ahead, he slowed the sorrel to a walk, jacked a cartridge into his Winchester, and held it at port arms, fully cocked. The reins drooped loosely from the fingers of his left hand.

Velasquez didn't know where the other shooters were, so he decided to rush Ness's hideout, trusting his friend not shoot him by mistake.

He released the cocked hammer of the Winchester and slid it back into its saddle scabbard. Pulling one of his nickel-plated Peacemaker Colts from its ornate holster, he plucked a .45 shell from his gunbelt to feed the empty chamber. He knew accurate shooting was difficult from the back of a running horse, but felt he could control the pistol better than the rifle.

He touched his rowels to the belly of the stallion, and the horse leaped from a sedate walk to a flag-tailed run in three strides. Velasquez watched west, searching for the rifleman who'd fired on Ness. He saw the horse first, ground-tied near a scraggly juniper. A man scrambled up the hill toward the horse.

Velasquez snapped a shot at him. The man ducked behind the horse, laid his rifle across the saddle, and aimed at the speeding sorrel.

Velasquez triggered two more shots at the man, missing both times. Smoke billowed from the rifle and the slug whipped through the air near Velasquez's ear. The sorrel thundered on over the rise, and Velasquez saw the old cabin where Ness hid out. The Mexican turned in the saddle to fire at the horseman and, as his bullets kicked up dust, the man clambered aboard the brown horse and spurred it east toward Saint Johns.

Velasquez hauled the sorrel to a stiff-legged, hopping stop at the door of the cabin. Ness Havelock stood there nonchalantly, pistol in hand.

'*Buenas tardes, amigo. Que tal?*' Velasquez said with a toothy grin.

''Bout time you got here,' Ness responded.

CHAPTER 11

The sock-footed bay carried me to Rancho Pilar, favoring his left hind leg all the way. We went straight to the bunkhouse after caring for the horses. The *vaqueros* slept, undisturbed by our arrival.

Just before the sun topped the hills to the east, a knock sounded on the door. 'Ness Havelock, are you in there?' Rita's voice had a hard edge.

Emilio chuckled. 'I think you should answer, *amigo*. She will not go away.'

'Ness!'

'I'm coming.' I pulled on my trousers and reached for my shirt.

'Good.' Her footsteps faded toward the hacienda.

'So what am I supposed to do?' I asked Emilio.

'Is it not clear? You must follow the *señorita* to the hacienda.' Again Emilio chuckled, and several of the *vaqueros*, now awake, joined in.

'*Señor* Havelock. *Gracias a Dios* you have returned to Rancho Pilar,' said one. 'With each passing day while you were gone, the *señorita* grew shorter and shorter of temper,

123

angel though she is.'

I struggled into my boots, not noticing my wound as much as I did the day before. Stepping to the commode, I splashed water on my face to clear the cobwebs from my sleep-addled brain, and ran my wet fingers through my hair.

'Emilio, I don't reckon that gunshot bay should be rode much. Could you ride to Saint Johns for my buckskin? And perhaps pick up my saddle-bags at the Higgins House?'

'It just so happens that I have business in Saint Johns,' Velasquez said. 'And I would be more than happy to bring your horse back with me.'

'Good. Then I'll go to the RP Connected tomorrow.'

Angry footsteps came from the direction of the hacienda. I hurriedly opened the door before Rita could pound on it. She stood there with the morning sun haloing her hair, fist raised, and eyes snapping. God, she was beautiful.

'Looking for me?' I asked.

'*Si*. For you, *señor*. You will follow me.' She turned on her heel and marched back to the hacienda. She'd gotten nearly halfway before she realized I was not behind her. She stamped her foot.

'Johannes Havelock. What must I do to get you to come into the hacienda?'

'You could try "please".'

She looked like she might choke. But after struggling with it for a moment, she got it out. *'Por favor, Señor* Havelock. Please.'

'I'll be right there.' I shut the door and returned the towel to its peg. When I opened the door again, she was standing there with her fists on her hips and her arms akimbo. 'Now are you ready, *señor?'*

'I am.'

She strode across the yard in long angry steps, but I sauntered, took my time.

'Buenos dias, Señor Havelock.' Paloma Javez greeted me with customary cheer.

'Morning, Paloma.'

'Ness, come,' Rita demanded. She took me down the long hall to the end room, the *dispensario* I'd heard her call it. Old Mujer, the witch and healer, sat there grinding her concoctions with mortar and pestle.

'Remove your shirt,' Rita commanded.

I took the shirt off. A large spot of dried blood spread across the back.

'Lie down here, please,' Rita said. Her expression had softened at the sight of the blood.

I lay down on my right side. The surface of the counter was cool against my skin. Rita slipped the lower blade of a large pair of scissors under the bandage on the entry wound and snipped it apart. The pad came away cleanly and the lips of the wound were closed over and healing well. The pad on the exit wound was glued to my back with old blood. Rita soaked it with warm water and pried it carefully away.

'*Gracias a Dios*,' she breathed. 'It is healing. Oh, Ness. I was so worried. You never take care of yourself, and I thought the wound might be rotting again.'

The old crone took hammer and tongs to that exit wound, at least that's what it felt like. She cleaned the wound good and slathered another coating of aloe and herbs on it.

'*Bueno*,' she announced, and left the bandaging to Rita.

Once I was bound up tight, I felt pretty good. That bullet of Gatlin's wasn't gonna hold me back much longer.

'Young Ruel Gatlin was here two nights ago,' Rita said.

'Gatlin? What for?'

'He brought the bodies of Cesar Ramirez and the shepherd boy Aldo home. He said they were killed for no good reason. Cesar was shot in the heart, but Aldo died when someone forced something red hot through his eye and into his brain. Their families mourn. Padre Juan Bautista blessed the bodies and we buried them yesterday.'

I could find no words. The two shepherds had saved my life, and died because they helped me. Suddenly, the war smoldering around Saint Johns got very personal. Anger began to burn deep in my gut.

'Rita,' I said, 'I make a vow. Whoever took the lives of Cesar and Aldo will taste death. I will see to it.'

She looked alarmed. 'No, Ness. No more killing.'

Rita held out a loose white shirt. 'This is Miguel's. He is still away at Santa Fe. I am sure he would not mind if you wore it. *Por favor.*'

I accepted the shirt. My shoulders were wider than Miguel Pilar's, but the shirt was cut loose and fit fine.

'Come,' Rita said. 'Paloma's delicious breakfast awaits.'

Sitting across the table from Rita Pilar felt mighty good. And the breakfast smells set my mouth to watering. We ate Paloma's tortillas and eggs and chorizo sausage, seasoned with fresh salsa and downed with cool goat's milk. The food was excellent, as always, but I tasted little as I ate, for my eyes constantly strayed to Rita and my heart galloped at the nearness of her. If only I were in a position to seek the hand of this beautiful woman. As it was, I stole a few moments of bliss just in being near her.

'Ness Havelock, why do you keep looking at me?' Her voice was low and warm.

'I keep wondering when you're going to jump up and take a bite outa my ear. You're a

127

scary woman, Rita Pilar. And I'm just a sore saddle tramp. There's no way I can stand up to you when you get mad.' I smiled.

Her eyes sparked. 'Then you must take better care of yourself. At least your wound is healing properly. Except for one small tear.'

'It feels a lot better.'

'Stay here, Ness. Rest. No one can bother you here,' she pleaded. I dearly wanted to spend a few quiet days in her company, but that could not be.

'*Buenos dias, señorita,*' said Emilio Velasquez as he entered the kitchen.

Rita stood and went to the stove. '*Tortillas y huevos, señor, con salsa. Esta bien?*'

'Stupendous,' he replied in English. 'As Ness would say, I have so much hunger that I could devour my own *caballo*.' Emilio laughed. Rita brought the eggs and tortillas, and for a while there was no conversation. She went back to the stove for the coffee pot.

'I'll ride for Saint Johns now, Ness,' said Emilio. He sipped coffee from a pottery cup. 'You should rest. Perhaps get some more sleep. Nothing helps the body to heal better than sleep. I will return with your buckskin horse and your belongings before the sun sets, I promise.'

I chuckled at his seriousness. 'Be careful, Emilio. Any of Wilson's men could decide to shoot you from ambush just because you kept Baldy Fontelle from stretching my hide.'

'I will prance my mount down the middle of Commerce Street. Let them shoot if they dare. They shall find that Emilio Velasquez does not die so easily.'

I put a hand on his arm. 'You're a friend, Emilio.'

'Rest, *mi amigo*. I shall soon return.' He swept from the house and moments later the thunder of his sorrel stallion's hoofs said he'd gone to get Buck.

'There goes a man to ride the river with,' I said to no one in particular, 'and the desert, and the mountains.'

I faced Rita again. 'Would you do me a favor, Rita? Show me the graves of Cesar and Aldo, please. I'd like to pay my respects.'

'But they are buried in the *cementerio* behind the mission.'

'Would you take me there?'

'But, Ness, you should rest.'

'Dear Rita. Two fine men died because they helped a gunshot gringo. Because of them, I live. Because of me, they're dead. The least I can do is pay my respects. Perhaps we could go in your buggy. Will you do that for me?'

Tears welled in the corners of her eyes. 'I will take you.'

A dapple-gray with black legs, mane and tail pulled the light buggy smartly, and we reached the mission too soon because I wanted to ride there beside Rita forever. Padre Juan Bautista waited at the front door of the chapel.

'*Buenos dias, padre,*' Rita said. 'Ness came to pay respects to Cesar Ramirez and the boy Aldo Baca.'

'Of course,' the padre answered. 'But a candle for their souls in the chapel before, no?'

Rita bought two long candles, and we lit them from the flames of those still burning and stood them in their own wax – for the souls of poor Cesar and Aldo. Rita steepled her hands before the altar and curtsied. I stood there like a lump, sad to the core that those good men had died.

'Come,' she said, and led the way to the graves.

They lay buried with their families. The two fresh graves were easy to spot. Neither had a headstone, just wooden crosses with their names and dates of death.

'When will they get headstones, *padre?*'

'Maybe never, my friend. The families of these sheepherders are not wealthy. And headstones are not first among the things that are important to them. God saw Cesar and Aldo fall, and He has taken them into His bosom. That is enough.'

'I will see that they get headstones,' I said. 'A hundred years from now, people should know that these men gave their lives for another.'

Rita touched my arm, her eyes again filled with tears. On the way home, she sat close beside me, and I was sorely tempted to pull her even closer. God, it was agony being next to her, and yet so far away.

'It is a good thing you do, Ness Havelock, the headstones,' she said.

'That's the least I can do.'

'And what about me, Ness? Am I too to receive only a headstone as a token of your affection? Sometimes you feel so distant I could die.'

'We've been down that trail before, Rita. I'm not the man for you.'

'Stop saying that! My heart tells me you are the one. Can you not understand that? I don't want to spend another two years wondering if you are dead or alive.'

'Rita. Rita. Rita. Do you think your father, the great Don Fernando Pilar, would ever allow his precious daughter to wed a shiftless wanderer? Not likely. Let's leave well enough alone.'

'*Madre de Dios*, Johannes Havelock. You make me so angry sometimes. Why can you not get it through your slow-moving brain that my father is not the one who has lost his heart to you? It is not he who decides who I will or will not wed.'

For a moment I was tempted, but I knew

I would only hurt her in the long run. I had to keep my distance. Even if it killed me.

'The drive to the mission tired me more than I thought,' I fibbed when we got back to the hacienda. 'I think I'll go to the bunkhouse and rest.'

Suddenly she was all concerned. 'But of course. How thoughtless of me. I will call you when the evening meal is ready.'

In the bunkhouse, her words lingered and her image seemed imprinted on my eyelids. Still, I slept. Then the figure of young Ruel Gatlin seemed to come at me out of the sun. I felt a hand on my shoulder and reacted instinctively, grabbing it, slipping my thumb beneath the thumb of the hand, and using my other hand to apply pressure at the wrist. Emilio Velasquez dropped to his knees beside the bunk.

'*Por favor, amigo*. That is my best gun hand, and how am I to protect you if it is broken?'

I released him. 'You should know better than to sneak up on a man.'

'Sneak? I came in through the door, and I made enough noise to wake the dead. Never have I known you to sleep so soundly. When you refused to answer my voice calling your name, what could I do but shake you? Now, you are awake, no?'

'Whaddaya want?'

'Do you not want to greet your fine buckskin horse after so many days away from him? Do you not want to don your new Stetson hat, which you left lying on the street in front of the newspaper office? Do you not want to clean and oil the fine Winchester rifle I brought from the Higgins House? If you are not interested, please go back to sleep.'

'Get outa here. I'll be out directly.'

Emilio Velasquez laughed, and left me in the dusk of the bunkhouse. I pulled on my boots and splashed water on my face at the commode. I dried my hands on the flour sack towel and went outside to greet Buck.

The horse stood on the other side of the corral, bumping noses with a sorrel in the far pen. I whistled and his ears pricked. Another whistle brought him trotting across the corral to get his ears scratched. He looked sleek and fit, ready to take me to the RP Connected or anywhere else I wanted to go.

'Buck, you old cayuse. How ya doing?' We'd traveled the Trail for nearly three years, and the buckskin still had many a mile left in his great muscles. Tomorrow we'd ride again.

'Emilio, where's that rifle you were talking about?'

'Use your eyes, *amigo*. The Winchester stands next to the tack shed with your saddle and saddle-bags.'

I was all of a piece again. I didn't have

much to call my own, just a decent saddle, a good bedroll and slicker, an accurate Winchester and extra shells for it and my .44 Colt, the clothes on my back, an extra shirt, a long lariat, a two-quart canteen, and a one-man coffee pot. And my gray flat-crowned Stetson.

I took up the rifle and jacked a shell into the chamber. The action worked smooth and fast.

'What are you smiling about, gringo?' Emilio's voice had a chuckle in it.

'I don't have much, my friend, but it's good to have it all back again. *Muchas gracias* to you.'

'*De nada, amigo,*' he said.

'Something smells mighty good,' I said. 'Wonder if chow's about ready.'

Emilio shrugged, but led the way to the hacienda. I followed with the Winchester tucked under my arm.

'*Hola, señores,*' Paloma said as we entered. 'The meal will be ready soon. Please wait in the great room, *por favor.*'

Don Fernando sat in his favorite chair. I glanced around for Rita, but she wasn't there.

'*Señor* Havelock, *Señor* Velasquez. How good it is to have you here. And how are you healing, *señor?*' he extended his hand to me. 'My daughter tells me Ruel Gatlin shot you.'

'He did, Don Fernando, but thanks to

Cesar Ramirez and Aldo Baca, I live. And thanks to Rita and Old Mujer, my wounds heal.' I stepped forward to shake his hand. 'And thanks to my friend Emilio Velasquez of Ciudad Juarez, I was not shot dead by those who killed Cesar and Aldo.'

Rita poked her head in. 'Our meal is ready. Please join us,' she said.

Don Fernando stood, and we followed him to the dinner table.

Paloma Javez had prepared a feast. Tamales. Chilis filled with goat cheese and swimming in thick broth. Shredded dried beef called *machaca*. Mounds of hot *tortillas de harina*. Fresh *salsa*. A pottery bowl of mashed pinto beans. I stuffed myself without reserve. Paloma watched with approval.

Little conversation interrupted the meal.

Then Don Fernando spoke. 'I sent Miguel to Santa Fe to get papers that show the Pilar Grant is recognized by New Mexico, Arizona, and the United States of America.'

'Cesar and Aldo were not killed by sheep haters,' I said. 'They were simply murdered. It does not follow that Rancho Pilar will be attacked.'

'Perhaps you are right.' The white-haired don seemed lost in thought.

'*Señor* Havelock,' he said, eventually, 'may I see you in the library after supper?'

CHAPTER 12

Buck had carried me a good distance toward the RP Connected by the time the sun cleared the eastern hills. I had a good breakfast under my belt and the day of rest did wonders for the holes Ruel Gatlin put in my hide.

I felt good, once again on the hurricane deck of my buckskin. Few cayuses in the country could match him for an easy stride and a quick pace. Me and Buck just naturally fit together.

A good deal of water had trickled downstream since Isom Dart first told me Roland Prince needed help. Now, finally, I was going to see him.

The buckskin's fast pacing soon had me in sight of the RP Connected. The ranch was a long skinny swatch that bordered Rancho Pilar on the south and Preston Hanks's Claymore outfit on the north, with the house located on a table of land that gave it a clear view all around. No one has ever planted a tree on that little mesa, so the headquarters was just a cluster of house, bunkhouse, barn, stables, tack-room, granary, and corrals.

The only exception to the rawhide look of

the place was a dozen or so fruit trees that grew down off the mesa below the small seep that supplied water.

Ace Cruger stood out front of the house as I rode up. 'The boss in?' I asked.

'Not sure he's interested in seeing any ghosts,' Ace said warily.

'I'm alive and well, after being shot and chased all over this end of the Colorado Plateau.'

'Rumor had you dead.'

'I've been rumored dead before. But those rumors were wishful thinking on the part of the shooters.'

'Ruel Gatlin was here with Harlow Wilson this morning.'

'Looking for me?'

'Riding shotgun, he said. Fontelle and them was off somewhere on Wilson's business.'

'Your boss in?'

'Yeah, he's in.'

'Cruger, you're getting to be like a mother hen in your old age. Last I heard, Roland Prince didn't need no mothering. You stay here. He'll call on you if he needs you.'

Cruger stood back as I dismounted.

'Be obliged if you'd water my horse,' I said. 'He's come a ways today.' I mounted the steps to the porch and rapped at the screen door.

'Come in, Ness.' Prince's strong voice from

137

the dark interior was not like a crippled man at all. He sat at a roll-top desk in the far corner of the room. I crossed the room with an outstretched hand. His white hair had been dark blond in the days when he'd hauled me out of the Sonora Desert more dead than alive. A mite over six-one he'd stood, on two strong legs, with a laugh to match his big broad shoulders. And not even the deadly desert of Sonora could cut him down.

He didn't get up, but the hand that met mine was firm and the grip strong.

'How's the world treating you?' I asked.

'Terrible. Never worse.' He chuckled. 'And that's no joke.'

'You've taken on some pretty tall odds over the years. How's this any different?'

'The desert's a killer, Ness, but it ain't a schemer. And gunmen can only pull triggers. This time I'm up against something different, and I can't see where it's coming from.' Prince frowned.

'That why you sent for me?'

Prince looked me in the eye. 'Ness, if there's an honest man in the world, you're him. And I need one honest man on my side.'

'One thing I need to know, Roland. You in cahoots with Harlow Wilson? To my way of thinking, he's about the lowest thing that walks on two legs.'

'Sometimes a man's got no choice.'

'Wilson coming in partners with you?'

'Not if I can help it.'

'Then just what do you have in mind for me to do?'

'Maybe there ain't nothing you can do, Ness,' he said. 'Things're grinding down.'

'You giving up?'

He stared at me for a moment, and I saw a flicker of determination in his eyes. Then the light died. 'Ness,' he said. 'I don't know how much longer I'll be alive. Look.' He pulled a handful of papers from a desk drawer. They looked the same as the charred note Emilio Velasquez had brought from Rancho Pilar. I picked one up.

CRIPPLED MEN DIE. YOUR TIME IS NIGH.

Another one read:

DEATH WILL BE GOOD FOR YOU CRIPPLE SOON.

'How long have you been getting these?'

'Month, month and a half.'

'And when did Harlow Wilson come to town?'

'Oh, he came the first time in March. Stayed at the Higgins House. Made a lot of noise about bringing a lot of stock into the country. The businessmen that call themselves the Saint Johns Ring figured Wilson'd be good for the town.'

'But when did he come to stay?'

'He bought the old Sturdevant place dirt cheap. Showed up with a dozen riders and five young boys. No cows, though.'

'When was that?'

'Couple of months ago.'

'And then the notes started showing up, right?'

Prince frowned. 'Well, not right away.'

'They start showing up before or after you and him got together?'

'After.'

'And you never made a connection?'

'He don't have to kill me.'

'Maybe he wants to.'

Prince remained silent.

'Roland, a boy named Ronnie Dunne died in my camp after Harlow Wilson horse-whipped him. Sid Lyle and his bunch tried to do me in with loads of double-o buckshot through Myra Beck's bedroom window, just because Preston Hanks got wind that you'd sent for me. And Ruel Gatlin put lead in me a few days back, wanting to avenge his brothers.' I pulled up a side chair and sat across from my ailing friend.

'Isom Dart told me you needed help. I owe you my life and more after Sonora, but damned if I can see what to do.'

Roland raised both his hands in surrender.

'Take 'er easy, Ness,' he said.

'I'd take it red hot and sizzling if I just knew what I was grabbing hold of.'

'I get them notes, Ness. I'm in debt just keeping this outfit going. And I've got a foreman who runs the place any way he feels like. I sometimes think he's letting my stock mix with Preston's Herefords on purpose, trying to keep the Claymore mad at the RP Connected.'

'Who's your foreman?'

'Kenigan Zane.'

'Zane? I know him from the Trail. Want I should have a word with him?' I asked.

Prince looked hopeful.

'I'll do what I can,' I said.

'The RP Connected's not all that big, Ness. Nine thousand head, more or less, and the remuda. That's all I been able to build since Sonora. And since I got shot, it ain't been easy. People see that I can't walk without crutches and that makes 'em think I'm weak.'

'Roland, when a man talks about dying, the turkey buzzards come flocking in, waiting for him to rot.'

'I know that, Ness. They're already here. The RP Connected ain't got all that much patented land, but I've got Cotton Creek and a slice of the Little Colorado, and the seep behind the house. I'd do OK if I was let be.'

'Like I said, what do you want me to do?'

'I'd be obliged if you'd have a word with Zane. He's got a small crew out gathering cows.'

'Already? They oughta graze two more months.'

'Ness. I gotta have cash. I got a note coming due.'

I said nothing.

'And Ness,' he continued. 'I'm small fry. There's something a lot bigger under foot. Maybe you can find out what it is.'

'I can try. I move a little slower with Gatlin's bullet hole in me, but I move.'

'Were I you, Ness Havelock, I'd keep an eye out for Ruel Gatlin. You may think he's gunning for you because of an old grudge, but Ace Cruger tells me Harlow Wilson's paying him to kill you.'

Ruel Gatlin a paid killer? Yet he'd refused to shoot me in Cesar Ramirez's camp. I wondered how much I was worth to Wilson. And why.

'Ness,' Roland said. 'I done as best I could here. Whatever happens, I'd hope the RP Connected goes on. I never found a woman who'd get hitched with me so I have no kids. But I've ridden with good men like you, and maybe that's all a man can ask for. I've done what I could for this spread, and if I have my way, Harlow Wilson won't get it.'

'I'll keep nosing around,' I said.

Prince raised his head, a startled look on his face as if he'd forgotten I was standing there. 'All right,' he said. 'Let me know what turns up.' He sat with his head bowed over the desk as I let myself out the front door.

Roland Prince hadn't told me everything he knew. But I had a bullet hole in my side that said Ruel Gatlin wanted my hide, and now I knew he was getting paid to do the job.

Ace Cruger had my buckskin staked out under the apple trees. I walked down off the little mesa rather than whistle at him to bring the horse up. Water trickled out of the seep, filling a basin where stock could drink. I wondered if Roland had rigged a pump to take water to the kitchen. Women like pumps in the kitchen, but there was no woman on the RP Connected. In fact, I didn't see anyone around.

I picked a green apple from one of the trees and polished it on my sleeve. I bit into it, slurping the juice and savoring its tartness.

'Young Gatlin favored green apples,' Cruger said.

Something in his voice made me ask, 'You favor him?'

Cruger squinted at me. 'Ness, that youngster's got more between his ears than folks might think. He sees what goes on over to the Pitchfork, and he hears the whiffle

Wilson spouts. I'm thinking he's his own man and don't take kindly to being told what to do. He's just a whisker of a boy, but I'm thinking Ruel Gatlin's got a rod of steel down his backbone.'

'Hear Wilson's paying him to gun me.'

'That may be. But when the chips are down, I'd bet on Gatlin making up his own mind.'

Cruger could be right. Gatlin hadn't finished me off when I was down. And he'd not let Destain shoot me. But fact remained, I had killed his three brothers in Telluride, and he had vowed revenge. 'I don't say you're wrong, Ace. But I think I'll just stay clear of that youngster. He put lead through me and I'm not yet healed. I'd just as soon he didn't come a-shooting right now.'

Cruger chuckled. He led the buckskin over and handed me the reins.

'Where's Zane at?' I asked.

'Him and our other three riders are gathering cows.'

'Then why ain't you out helping?'

'Boss said to stick around. Keep my eyes peeled.'

'Roundup, huh? When'd they leave?'

'Sun-up. Took the old woman and the chuck wagon. They ain't traveling too far today, I'd say. Why?'

'Thought I'd have a word with Kenigan Zane. Know him from the Trail.'

144

Ace Cruger scuffed at the grass with a boot, wiping off a bit of manure. 'Zane's as good a man with cows as they come, I reckon. But lately he's had a burr under his saddle. Don't know what it is, but he's sure on his high horse.'

'I'll ride out and see if I can find them. Now's as good a time as any to talk with them cowboys.' I swung up on the buckskin. He was rearing to go and pranced a step or two. I held him with a tight rein. 'Where at do you figure they'll start rounding up the beeves?'

'They'll cross the river at Hartley's Ford and start down the south bank of Cotton Creek. But they'll camp tonight on the west bank of the Little Colorado, I'd say.'

'So long, Ace. You keep an eye on Roland Prince. He's counting on you.'

Cruger touched a finger to his hat as Buck pranced down the road off the mesa. I let the horse out into a long lope and we covered ground. Still, I made the camp on the Little Colorado River after dark, and hailed the camp-fire from some way out. Kenigan Zane answered.

'Ride in easy, stranger, and keep your hands where I can see 'em.'

I walked Buck into the firelight.

'Johnny Havelock. I'll be damned. Ain't seen you since, when? Brown's Hole? Hear they're calling you Ness these days.' Zane's voice sounded friendly, but he kept the Winchester saddle gun pointed in my direction.

'You don't have to point that thing at me, Zane. I ain't about to get into no shootout with RP Connected riders.'

He snorted. 'What there is of us.'

'Short handed?'

'Three cowboys, me, and the old woman,' he said.

'Who's flinging the hash?'

'Dagan.'

I laughed. Snuffy Dagan was well-known on the Trail for his skill with a dutch oven. 'You're not hurting if Dagan's your old woman. You'll gain pounds on this gather.' I stepped down from the buckskin and Zane's rifle muzzle followed. The Winchester made me nervous. It was cocked, and Zane surely had a cartridge in the chamber.

'Mind if I spend the night?'

Zane hesitated. What was he worried about? Why'd he keep that rifle pointed in my direction?

'You're welcome, Ness,' he said finally. 'Put your horse on the picket line and come have some of Dagan's good grub.'

I did. And it was. Dutch-oven-baked steaks with saleratus biscuits and lumpy-dick gravy. I ate more'n my share.

'Dagan,' I said to the wizened man in the flour-sack apron, 'you cook like an angel. You'd make someone a right good wife.'

146

'Havelock, you keep a civil tongue in your head or you'll get no breakfast.'

I raised my hands and laughed. 'I surrender. Just wanted you to know this is almighty good grub, Dagan.'

'Now that your belly's full, come meet the men,' Zane said. 'The tall drink of water's Sandy Klieg. He's been working for us from the start. The one in the middle with the Montana hat is Timothy Underwood. We just call him Montana. And the kid's Evan Brown. This is his first roundup. His folks farm over to Shumway.' The three cowboys nodded from the far side of the fire.

I went over and shook their hands.

'Been a while, Montana. Gave up on the Hashknife, did you?'

'That leg never did heal up right, Mr Havelock. RP Connected suits me fine.'

'You boys'll do all right if you listen to Kenigan Zane. No better man with cows.'

I turned to Zane. 'You feed them any stories about driving up the Goodnight-Loving?'

The ears of that Brown youngster perked right up. 'You drove cows up the Goodnight-Loving Trail, boss? Man! That's cowboying!'

'Kid, driving on the trail to Colorado ain't something a man in his right mind would do. Back then, I could drive cows or I could go to begging. No other choice. The drives

147

was cold. And gawdawful dangerous. Them longhorns was mean. The straw boss was meaner. And many's the friend I buried on the way. I was lucky. Now let it rest.'

The boy ducked his head, but his eyes were shining. He was gathering cattle with a real drover. Zane had just climbed a few notches on the kid's list of heroes.

'Zane,' I said, 'wonder if I could have a word with you?' I walked out of the firelight toward the river. I could hear his footsteps behind me, and wondered if he was carrying that cocked Winchester. But I didn't turn, even when I got to the ford. I reached down and scraped up a handful of pebbles and stood there throwing them into the water, one at a time. Zane was silent, standing just behind me.

'Zane, we both been up and down the Trail from Bozeman to Ciudad Juarez. And neither of us is a wanted man. From all I've heard and from all I know about you, you're a man of your word. And in my book, that includes riding for the brand as long as the boss is honest.'

Zane joined me, tossing pebbles into the river.

'I rode over to talk to Preston Hanks at the Claymore the other day,' I went on. 'He's a mighty worried man. He went out on a limb to get those Englishmen to invest in his place so he could bring white-face cattle into the country. Naturally, he wants to keep them separate.'

'Oughta fence 'em then,' Zane muttered.

'That day's coming, Zane. But Roland Prince would take it kindly if you'd do your best to keep RP Connected stock from mixing with Claymore cows. And as Prince is a friend of mine, I'd appreciate it, too. Cows ain't a good reason to fight. What d'ya say?'

Zane flung another pebble at the river and watched the silvery splashes it made skipping across the water in the moonlight.

'Seems to me the boss went soft after that bushwhacker crippled him,' Zane said. 'The Claymore is a lot bigger'n us. Seems to me they're the ones should be watching out for their own stock.'

'Zane, you know something fishy is going on in these parts. So I'd like to ask you a personal favor – not that I'm in any position to ask favors – but would you watch out for RP Connected cows? Keep 'em from wandering onto Claymore range? I'm trying to get to the bottom of things and your help would sure be appreciated.'

He threw another pebble. 'OK, Ness. I can do that. We got to put fifteen hundred head together to sell, the boss says, so I'll get 'em off the north sections.'

'Obliged, Zane. And you got to give Prince the benefit of the doubt. He's still a tough man.'

'Yeah, I 'spose,' Zane said, but he didn't sound convinced.

After a healthy breakfast of side meat and biscuits, washed down with two big cups of coffee, me and Buck set off for Saint Johns. As we topped the rise above Cotton Creek, I saw smoke in the bottoms, enough for at least a dozen fires.

CHAPTER 13

Greenhorns camped in the bottoms of Cotton Creek, with four wagons scattered about and a bunch of fires burning. Me and Buck rode off the rise to see what was going on.

Westerners would have had me covered with rifles and pistols, cocked and ready, but I saw no weapons, even though the clamor of the buckskin's hoofs over the rocky ground caught the attention of everyone in camp. Open, honest faces watched me ride down the hill, and that bothered me. After all, I coulda been some strong-arm out to take whatever those poor folks had.

As I got closer, I noticed their stock. Poorer horses I'd not seen in a long time, and the wagons left more than a lot to wish for. The camp had few utensils, it seemed. Folks'd wrapped coils of dough on sticks and stuck them in the ground by the fires to bake. On the trail, we do the same, but no camp cook worth his beans ever baked bread that way.

A young man stepped forward as I got closer, and I reined Buck in a couple of yards shy of him.

'Howdy,' I said. 'I'm Ness Havelock.'

His eyes lit up. 'Havelock?' he said, and then let go with a stream of talk in some language I never heard before.

I held up my hand. 'No. No. Wait. I don't understand a word you're saying.'

He hesitated, then spoke again. 'Havelock is a name known to us in our country. I thought you would know our speech.'

'And where might the old country be?' I asked.

'It is far across the sea. Norge, Norway in your language.' His accent was one I'd not heard before, but I could make out what he said.

'What brings you here?'

'*Ja*. We come to our new home. We gave all our money for new homes in this land.'

'And what's your name?' I asked.

'*Ja*. I am called Leif Hakansen.'

'And these people?'

'Some are family. Some are from our village. Please, one question?'

I nodded.

'Is the land in this country really free? There is no land for us where we came from. We want land. We came to farm.'

I didn't know quite what to say. 'Well. Land is free. And again it ain't free.'

He looked puzzled. 'Ain't?'

'Not. Not free. Some land's not free.'

He looked sad for a moment. Then he

brightened. 'Some free,' he repeated. 'Some not free. *Ja*. We want some free land, please.'

I found myself liking this tall blond man who stood there twisting his cloth cap in a pair of hands that knew work.

A young boy ran up to Hakansen and said something. Hakansen looked embarrassed. 'My wife says be polite. Please. Join us to eat.'

From the looks of things, these clod-busters didn't have the extra grub to be offering me any. But I had coffee; I always carried a bag of Arbuckles.

'I ate early this morning,' I said, 'but I would enjoy a cup of coffee. Would you join me?' I reached into my saddle-bags and took out the sack of coffee beans. 'I'll supply the coffee.'

Hakansen grinned. 'I like coffee,' he said.

I climbed off Buck and tied him to a wagon wheel. The Norway man led me to one of the fires, where a woman almost as tall as him tended the bread baking on sticks. I saw at once that there was no coffee pot, so I went back to Buck and got my little pot. Four cups was all it held, but I'd make coffee all morning if that's what it took. Something told me these were good folks. Solid. The kind a raw country needs.

I smashed the coffee beans with the butt of my Colt and every adult in camp had a cup. The morning turned out better'n most.

Leif spoke English best, but everyone came up to greet me and thank me for the coffee. I couldn't help but smile.

Hunkered down by the fire, I worked at finding out just what these folks were up to. Slowly the story began to make sense. They'd left the old country in March, before first thaw. They'd hoped to find their land and start farming by summer. But the ship had trouble and took nearly two months to cross the ocean. Three babies were born on the way over. One survived.

Once in New York, they'd nowhere to go. They found no free land in the east, and they had very little money. They saw the poster in June. Free land in Arizona, it read. Transportation and equipment, $100 for adults, children free.

'We paid all our money, except for a few ... what do you say ... pennies? We didn't have one hundred for each adult, but the agent took one thousand and eight hundred and fifty-three dollars,' Hakansen said. 'We got broke-down wagons and old horses, but we are here. And you say some land is free.'

How they wanted land. But right now, they were on the RP Connected, and Roland Prince wouldn't take kindly to pumpkin rollers squatting on his water.

'It's summer now, Leif,' I said, 'and moving toward fall. You'll need money to get through the winter. Any of you blacksmith or carpenter?'

Hakansen nodded. 'Since I was very small, I worked with wood. In the old country, I made tables and chairs and spinning wheels.' Then his face fell. 'But I could not bring the heavy tools.'

'Anyone else?'

'Kort Bjornsen is a worker of iron,' he said, indicating the sturdy fellow standing nearby.

'You two catch horses and come with me.'

Leif Hakansen and Kort Bjornsen mounted two of the old plow horses and followed me toward Saint Johns. I could tell by the way they sat the plugs that butts would be sore long before day's end.

Come noon, I fished biscuits and bacon from my saddlebags and made us each a bacon-biscuit sandwich. They had no canteens, so I shared my water with them.

'*Mange takk*,' Leif said, 'Thanks much in our Norwegian talk.'

Bjornsen said something to Leif. 'Your name Havelock is not uncommon in the old country,' he translated. 'Came you from Norway?'

'My pa said we was Norse,' I replied. 'Back three or four generations, one of my ancestors was a sea captain. Some called him a pirate. He's the one they called Havelock. I've heard it means sea warrior in the old tongue. I don't know if Norse means our

155

ancestor came from your country, but we have kept Norse names in the family. My name is Johannes. My brother is Garet. My father was Rothwell. And his father before him was Gunnar, a fighting man, they say.'

'Fine men of the sea come from Norge,' Leif said. 'I am happy to know you, Johannes Havelock.'

'Ness.'

'*Ja*. Ness.'

We rode into Saint Johns not long after noon. I led the Norwegians straight to Swede Lund's blacksmith shop. I climbed off the buckskin and looped his reins over the hitching rail. I motioned for the Norway men to do the same with their scrawny mounts, and we walked over to Swede's forge. He just kept working that hot iron while we stood there.

At last Swede shoved the piece in a bucket of water. A cloud of steam arose with the wet smell of hot iron. He laid the work back on the anvil and looked at us. 'Well?'

'My name's Ness Havelock,' I said, 'brother to Garet Havelock of the H-Cross ranch on Silver Creek.'

Swede nodded.

'Bjornsen here says he's a smithy. You have some work for him?'

Swede motioned to Bjornsen. The big Norwegian went to the bellows without a word and started pumping them with a pair of arms as thick as a grown man's thigh. Swede took some tongs and turned the work in the coals, making sure it heated to a uniform cherry red. Pulling the piece from the forge, Swede inclined his head toward the other hammer on the bench. Bjornsen took it up in his ham-like fist and stepped to the far side of the anvil. Swede hit the anvil twice with his hammer to set the rhythm, then those two big men took to pounding that piece of iron one after the other in perfect time. Each time he turned the work, Swede would hit the anvil twice and they'd take up their rhythm again. And before you'd know it, Swede was holding a perfect buggy spring in his tongs. The two had not said a single word to each other.

'Good,' Swede pronounced. 'One dollar a day.' Bjornsen looked at Leif, who spoke to him in Norwegian. The big man grinned. He stuck out a huge hand to Swede, who gripped it, sealing the deal.

'Let's go.' I swung up on the buckskin, and Leif got on the old plug of a workhorse a bit gingerly. I led the way across the bridge toward Concho. The long summer days gave us lots of daylight, but we still got to Erastus, the Mormon settlement near Concho, late in the afternoon. Those Norwegian settlers needed help, and if anyone could get them through the next weeks, it was the Mormons.

Elijah Taylor's place was at the edge of

town, and we rode up with the sun a couple of hours from the horizon. Taylor's kids saw us coming and had their ma out front by the time we reined our horses up at the house.

'Would Elijah be here, Sister Taylor?'

'He's over to the south forty, cutting hay. Should be back before dark, though.'

'This is Leif Hakansen, Sister Taylor. Elijah did me a favor not long ago, getting some wounded men from Twelve-Mile Knoll. Sure appreciate that.'

'We're taught to look out for our neighbors,' she said.

'Would it be all right if we rode over to speak to Elijah?'

'Of course.' She turned and hollered, 'Samuel. Samuel Taylor.'

In two minutes flat, a kid of nine or so in a floppy hat came skidding around the corner of the house. 'Whadja want, Ma?'

'Mother.'

The boy screwed up his face. 'What do you want, Mother?' he said.

'If children don't talk right to family, they can't speak properly when company comes,' Sister Taylor said. 'Samuel, you show Mr Havelock to the south forty, please.'

'Yes, ma'am,' he said, and broke into a run down the lane.

'Hey, Sam,' I called. He stopped. I motioned him over and took a foot from the stirrup.

'Come on up,' I said. 'Ol' Buck can ride double easy.'

The boy's face was one big smile as he grabbed my hand and I boosted him up behind. He directed us to a broad flat divided up into forty-acre squares. Some were planted in alfalfa, others grew corn or cabbages or pumpkins. Mormon men worked in many of the fields.

Half-a-dozen men and older boys swung scythes in Taylor's forty. They'd cut a good swath through the alfalfa but had nearly twenty acres left to mow. Elijah Taylor shouldered his scythe and walked over.

'Evening, Elijah,' I said. He seemed to bring the scent of new-cut hay with him. Sweat damped his shirt and streaked his face. His teeth flashed white in a sun-darkened face. Taylor stuck out his hand, and I got off the buckskin to shake it. He didn't ask what I wanted or why I'd come. He just stood there letting me take my own time.

'I'm here to ask for your help again, Brother Taylor.'

He nodded.

I motioned Leif over.

'This here's Leif Hakansen,' I said. 'Him and his folks just came from Norway. They're camped in the bottoms of Cotton Creek on the RP Connected. Brother Taylor, they're hurting. They've got nothing to cook with and precious little to eat. They don't have a place to settle, and they'll not find one soon. I know it's not for me to be asking – specially since I have nothing to give of my own – but I'd sure be obliged if you could help them.'

A smile crinkled Elijah Taylor's cheeks as he grasped Leif's hand. 'Glad to know you, Mr Hakansen. How many able men do you have in camp?'

Leif had his answer ready. 'Twelve grown men and seven boys who will soon be men,' he said.

'Do you know farming?'

Leif took a deep breath. '*Ja*. We are farmers. Good farmers. We came here to find farming land.'

'We have hay to cut, and when that's done, there'll be corn to bring in and shuck, and then the potatoes ... your help would be welcome.'

Leif grinned. 'We can work. We like to work.'

'I can use ten men. I can send a wagon for them tomorrow. They can board with us here in Erastus and go home Saturday evening to spend the Sabbath with their families,' said Taylor.

'*Mange takk*,' Leif said. 'We have our wagon. Ten men you say. We will come. We will work. *Mange takk*.'

'You two better stay at our place tonight,' Taylor said to me. 'If you don't mind home

160

cooking and sleeping in the hay loft, that is.'

'That's the best offer I've had in a long time, Elijah,' I said.

'We eat simple at night,' Taylor said, but the table was mounded high with fresh-baked bread, cool milk, butter, currant jam, wild honey, and slices of smoke-cured ham. After Taylor said grace, conversation fell off as we took after that good food, trying to keep up with the six Taylor youngsters.

By the end of the meal, Taylor had gotten Leif's story, and I found out the Norwegians had been brought to Arizona by the Mogollon Land and Mining Company. I'd never heard that name before.

Young Sam Taylor adopted Leif. Must have seemed exciting to the boy, having someone from across the ocean to talk with. The two of them went to the barn with an armload of quilts and blankets to make a bed for us on the loose hay.

'I want to thank you, Elijah,' I said, when Leif was out of earshot, 'for helping these folks.'

His eyes twinkled. 'We could give them food, Ness, but folks appreciate things more if they work to earn them. We can't pay cash for their labor, but we'll make sure part of the harvest is theirs.'

The pile of fragrant hay in the barn loft was good as Myra Beck's feather bed. And another night of good sleep took more of

161

the soreness out of the wound in my side. In the morning, while Leif and Sam were milking cows, I practiced pulling my Colt from its holster. The pistol came out OK, but I could tell the edge had gone off my gun work.

I had to start practicing again.

When the morning chores were done, Evina Taylor filled us up with flapjacks and butter and honey and milk fresh from the cows, along with long crinkly strips of smoked side meat.

'We'd better go with your wagon back to the Cotton Creek camp. Most of those folks don't speak our lingo, and Leif had better be there to make sure they all understand.'

Riding always gave me time to think, and these new immigrants changed the lie of the land in Apache County. They'd stick together and they'd work hard and they'd make a dent in county politics, no doubt. I wondered just who the Mogollon Land and Mining Company was. Leif had said six men on horseback had met them at the siding near Navajo Springs. The men'd had nothing to say, except for the leader, who didn't give his name. In their excitement over finally getting to the place where there was free land, the immigrants gratefully accepted the campsite offered by their guides.

I felt sure the Mormons and probably the Mexicans in Concho would help see them through the winter. And I could try to find the Mogollon Land and Mining Company and see what its intentions were toward these greenhorns.

Things for me to do were piling up mighty high. Help Roland Prince and Preston Hanks. Stand up to Ruel Gatlin one day soon. Stay clear of Baldy Fontelle and the Pitchfork riders, who'd pretend the fight at Twelve-Mile Knoll never happened.

And Don Fernando had asked a favor of me that night at Rancho Pilar. The old man had said, 'I know not how much longer I will be here, Ness Havelock. When I am gone, Miguel can handle the rancho. But Margarita? I worry about my daughter. And I would like you to take care of her when I am gone.'

His words astonished me, and the white-haired patriarch must have sensed my feelings. He just smiled and said, 'You know and I know that my daughter is committed to you, *mi amigo*, but I would like to hear that you are also committed to her. That's all a father can hope for.'

I stammered out my line about having nothing to offer her.

'Shame on you, Ness Havelock,' Don Fernando said. 'So many youngsters start with nothing. But they have a lifetime to build. And they have each other for strength. Will you not promise, my young friend?'

His words had given me not only the permission but the invitation to finally express my love to Rita. 'I promise, Don Fernando. With my life.'

Now, as we rode toward Cotton Creek, I wondered how I was going to keep that promise.

CHAPTER 14

I might've known Harlow Wilson had his fingers in the pie. There he was in the Norwegian camp, whacking a quirt against his leg and looking sideways at Leif's wife. Baldy Fontelle and three other Pitchfork riders sat their horses in a half circle behind Wilson. A fifth rider sat a blue roan horse under a cottonwood tree on the bank of the stream. Our eyes met and Ruel Gatlin's hand went back to grip his pistol. But he didn't draw.

Neither Elijah Taylor nor Leif Hakansen had weapons, and none of Leif's people were armed. I kept my hands on the saddle horn and hoped we could talk our way out of this one.

Taylor stopped his wagon when it reached the flat, and Leif and I rode on in. Leif and his wife, Ellisif, talked right lively, with Leif glancing at Wilson now and again. Wilson just smirked and whacked his leg with his quirt.

Finally Leif turned to face Wilson. 'I am Leif Hakansen,' he said. 'My wife says we paid you to get us free land.'

'That is correct,' Wilson said. 'And I told

her that the contract between you people and the Mogollon Land and Mining Company has been fulfilled.'

'Fulfilled?'

'Yes. That means we have done as promised.'

'Where is our land?'

'There are many places available for homesteading.' Wilson's tone galled me, I had to speak up.

'I should've known you was mixed up in this, Wilson,' I said. 'You've left these folks in the middle of another man's ranch without so much as a by-your-leave. Is that what this company of yours promised?'

'We agreed to bring them to the area around the head-waters of the Little Colorado River. That we have done. Now, it's up to them to find their own homesteads just like anyone else.' Wilson smirked again. 'I sent word to Roland Prince. I imagine he will visit soon.'

'You took near two thousand dollars from these people, Wilson. And all they got was rail fare, four broken-down wagons, and some mighty poor pulling stock. And you say you fulfilled your end of the bargain?'

'We did.'

I looked beyond Wilson to where Ruel Gatlin sat his roan beneath the cottonwood tree. 'Gatlin,' I called. 'I know you and me got a score to settle, but I'd take it kindly if

166

you'd let it slide today. There's women and children here and they don't need to start in this country with bleeding and dying. Can you do that?'

After a long moment, the kid took his hand off his gun and crossed it over the other one on his saddle horn.

I turned back to Wilson. 'I wish I knew a way to make you help these folks through the winter, but I can't see one. So why don't you take your gunnies back to Saint Johns so we can help these people get settled?'

Wilson and Fontelle exchanged glances. Wilson put on a bright smile. 'Of course, Havelock. Our pleasure.' The Pitchfork owner sauntered to his buggy and got in. Clucking to the twin gray fillies in the traces, he drove up the rise and out of sight, with his five riders following. Ruel Gatlin stopped his strawberry roan at the top of the rise. After a moment, he raised his hand in farewell, then galloped after the others.

'Leif,' I called. The tall Norwegian came with his tall wife.

'Right now your camp's on land belonging to a ranch called the RP Connected,' I explained. 'The owner's Roland Prince, and he's a friend of mine. I'll ask him to let you stay here until you find homesteads.

'Now, you gather ten men to help Elijah Taylor and get them on their way. But you stay here. When I get back from seeing

Prince, you and me are gonna to make this camp fit to live in. Savvy?'

'Savvy?'

I chuckled. 'That's a word we use in these parts to mean "understand".'

'Savvy?' he repeated, rolling the word on his tongue. 'I will remember it. And yes, I savvy.'

I walked over to Taylor. 'Leif's getting the men ready to go, Elijah,' I said. ''Preciate all you're doin' to help.'

'You act like these folks are family, Ness.'

'My pa said we was Norse by lineage, though my ma was Cherokee. Leif and them is from Norway, and they say Havelock's a name familiar to them. Maybe they are family, Elijah.'

I gathered up my buckskin's reins and led him to the creek along with Taylor's team. The horses drank deep of the clear water and went to cropping at the grass on the banks until Leif had the men ready to go. They wore cloth caps and clothes that had seen the long voyage over. The garments were neatly patched and clean. The men stood ready to do their part, and I felt a little pride in their gumption. Like they really were family.

'Why don't the Norwegians bring one of their wagons,' Taylor suggested. 'They may have some time to work on it during the week, and the horses could use some good grazing in one of our pastures.'

Leif got the men to hitch a team to one of the wagons, and as the procession left the camp, more than one wife's eyes grew misty.

I tightened Buck's cinch and stepped aboard. The hitch in my side was no more than a momentary tightening. Ruel Gatlin's bullet hole was well on its way to becoming two white scars to match the ones his brothers punched in me with their guns back in '79. I lifted my hand to Leif and set the buckskin's head toward the RP Connected, but in the back of my mind, I kept seeing that Gatlin kid with his hand on the butt of his gun. I knew from drawing and dry-firing in Taylor's loft that I was no match for Gatlin right now. Sure as snow flies in winter, he'd come gunning for me, and sure as spring comes after the snow, I'd better be ready. I made up my mind to start practicing with my Colt that very day.

We came to the fork and I reined Buck south toward the RP Connected. As yet, there was no sign of Roland Prince on his way to the Norwegian camp.

Once across Cotton Creek, the hills started rolling higher and higher toward the Blues. A cut ran eastward from the track, and it looked like a good place to practice with my hogleg.

I reined the buckskin into the cut and we rode through the scattered boulders along the bottom. Out of sight of the wagon track, I stepped off Buck and left him ground-tied. I pulled a box of shells from the saddle-bags and walked to a wide spot in the cut. A white splotch fifty or sixty feet away would do as a target, but first I had to loosen up and get used to dragging the Frontier .44 from its holster and bringing it into line.

I took the bullets from the cylinder and put them in my pocket, then faced the splotch with my feet about shoulder-width apart. *Now!* My right hand reached across my body for the handle of the Colt. The web of my thumb cocked the hammer as the Colt cleared the holster and my gently squeezing trigger finger dry-fired the gun as it lined up with the target. The moves were smooth and fast, but not nearly as quick as Ness Havelock ought to be. I replaced the Colt and drew and dry-fired again. And again.

I don't know how long I stood there drawing and firing, but along the way, my hand began to remember how to do it. I didn't have to think about it. The hand found the grip of the Colt without hesitation and the gun lined up with the splotch almost on its own. I dug the bullets from my pocket and put them back in the cylinder, along with an extra from the box to make six.

I returned the Colt to its holster, drew, and fired. Buck pricked his ears, but stood fast. Five more times I drew and fired, putting the Colt back after each shot. I shucked the spent shells from the Colt and replaced them with fresh cartridges, then put the gun in my holster, drew and fired all six bullets at the white splotch as fast as I could cock the hammer and pull the trigger. Lead whined off up the cut as the bullets smashed into the splotch and ripped chunks out of the clay. Gunsmoke drifted down the cut on the slight breeze. The buckskin snorted at the smoke as it wafted past.

Twice more I drew and fired all six bullets in rapid succession. After that, I went back to drawing and firing one bullet at a time.

I'd just triggered off my fourth bullet when a shot sounded off toward the RP Connected. Then another. And another. Three evenly spaced shots. A call for help. I jammed my Colt into its holster, picked up the box of shells, and hurried back to the buckskin. When someone's in trouble, a man naturally rides to help.

Buck picked his own way through the rubble at the bottom of the cut, but I urged him into a lope after we hit the wagon track. As we topped a rise, I saw a small basin fringed by low malpais where a saddled horse trotted in agitated circles near a buckboard. Two men lay on the ground nearby.

I spurred Buck into a run and soon recognized the men. Roland Prince was dead.

Part of his head was blown away where the bullet had exited above his right eye. His white hair stirred in the breeze and his eyes were open to the sun. The bleeding had stopped, and blue-tailed flies buzzed at the wound. I was out of the saddle and sprinting for Ace Cruger while my horse was still coming to a stiff-legged halt, He lay on the other side of the wagon track, curled up in a ball, his gun still in his hand.

'Ace!' I shook his shoulder and tried to turn him.

'Don't.' His voice was a murmur.

'Who was it, Ace? Who killed Roland?'

Ace was gutshot and the bullet had probably hit a lung. Blood bubbles formed as he struggled to breathe, coloring his gray lips and unshaven cheek.

'That you, Ness?' More bloody froth came with the words he choked out.

'It's me, Ace. You hang in there. You'll be all right.'

'I'm dead, Ness.' He groped for something to hang on to. 'Ness? You there, Ness?'

When I gripped his hand, he let out a long sigh and went limp. His hand still grasped mine.

At the thunder of hoofs I palmed my Colt without thinking. But Wilson's men were already there, and they carried saddle guns, cocked and ready. Harlow Wilson came in his buggy with Ruel Gatlin trailing behind

172

on his fine piebald roan.

Baldy Fontelle's rough words jolted me. 'Whadja have to kill them for, Havelock?'

'Me? Why would I kill my own friend?'

Wilson walked over, his bullwhip coiled over his shoulder. 'Give me the gun, Havelock. And Baldy, if he twitches, shoot. Hear me?'

'Come on, Havelock. Why'ncha make a move?' Fontelle dearly wanted to shoot me.

'Fontelle,' I said, trying to keep everyone calm. 'I'm going to let the hammer of this Colt down before I give it to Mr Wilson. So don't you or Destain shoot me because I move my thumb, OK?'

Fontelle nodded, but raised his rifle to his cheek.

I let the hammer down and stuck the grip out where Wilson could grab it. He took the gun and tossed it over by the buggy – no way to treat a good Colt.

'Give me the Bowie, too,' Wilson said, holding out his hand. There was nothing for me to do but snake the knife from its scabbard and hand it over, hilt first. Wilson tossed it after the pistol. He had a wicked glint in his eyes that I didn't like.

'Now, Havelock, when we rode up, you were holding a six-gun and two men were lying dead on the ground. Looks like you killed them.' Wilson chuckled. 'Turn around, Mr Havelock.'

I turned, facing away from the Pitchfork riders and their cocked rifles. A manila hoop dropped over my head and shoulders, and the roper pulled it up so's the lariat pinned my arms tight against my sides. He backed his horse, and I couldn't keep up. I fell back on my butt, legs spraddled out to give me some kind of balance. The rider kept the lariat tight.

Baldy Fontelle walked over with his hat tipped back and a smirk on his hairless face. He held two pigging strings with loops built into them. He slipped one hoop over my gun hand and drew it tight. He handed the loose end to Destain, and looped the other string over my left hand.

'Stand up, Havelock,' Fontelle ordered. But the feller on the other end of that lariat kept it tight.

'Can't,' I said, and he whacked me up side the head with a big open hand, knocking my hat flying.

'Move,' he said in a toneless voice.

Somehow I got to my knees before the rider jerked me onto my butt again. Fontelle gave me the flat of his hand from the other side. His hard fingers smashed my cheeks against my teeth, and I tasted the salt and copper of my own blood.

'Up,' he said, and jerked on a pigging string. By God, I tried, but that ranny on the end of the lariat jerked me onto my butt once more. Fontelle backhanded me again, but this time I was able to go with the slap, so it opened no more cuts in my mouth.

'Come on, hard man. Get up.' Fontelle loved to bully.

Destain laughed. 'He don't look so hard, Baldy. Looks like calf ready for branding.'

'On your feet, killer,' Fontelle said, and I tried again, moving quickly to get to my knees and working hard to make it to my feet. This time the roper let me get all the way up before he jerked on the lariat, setting me back on my butt.

Four Pitchfork hands laughed. Only Wilson was silent. And Gatlin.

Fontelle was getting set to lambaste me again when Wilson spoke. 'Let him up, Baldy. It's time for him to receive punishment more worthy of his crime.' Wilson stood over me, a smile on his face. 'Let's see how much of a man you are, Ness Havelock. I, Judge Harlow Wilson, sentence you to two-dozen lashes, less one. And then, for the murders of Roland Prince and Ace Cruger, you can hang by the neck until you are dead.'

My head jerked up. Wilson was gonna whip me. Then hang me. Without a judge or jury.

I spit blood. 'You got no right to sentence me,' I said. 'This ain't a court of law. Hanging me would be lynching, and the law would have you swinging right along with

175

me.' I was desperate. I had no desire to swing for the deaths of Ace and Roland. I didn't shoot them.

Wilson merely smiled again. 'Oh, I'm not going to lynch you, Havelock. I'm only going to punish you and turn you over to Sheriff Hubbell. Baldy, tie him to the buggy.'

Fontelle and Destain stretched me out, pulling on their pigging strings so my arms came away from my sides and the lariat slid up and settled around my neck. The ranny on the horse drew the rope up tight, just short of choking me.

'Come along, Havelock,' Fontelle said, pushing me toward the buggy. In a moment, I stood at its side, my nose pressed into the canvas top.

Fontelle kicked at my ankles. 'On your knees,' he growled.

I knelt.

Destain pulled the pigging string on my gun hand tight and tied it to the rear buggy wheel. Fontelle did the same on the left, securing the hard little rope to the front wheel. The strings bit into my wrists and pulled at my shoulder muscles.

'Remove his shirt,' Wilson ordered.

Fontelle pulled the tail of my shirt out of my trousers, ripped it up the back, and pushed it forward onto my arms.

'Well, well. What is this?' Wilson slipped a finger down my back bone to slide it beneath the muslin bandage that held the pad against the exit wound Gatlin's bullet put in me, then cold steel slipped between the muslin and my skin. He turned the blade and cut the bandage and it fell away. 'My, my,' he mocked. 'You've been shot. How tragic.' He gouged at the wound with a finger, and pain shot all the way to the top of my head.

'It seems to be healing well,' Wilson said gaily. 'Let's see how it holds up under the lash.'

I heard the rustle of the bullwhip as he slipped it off his shoulder. 'Stand back,' he warned the riders. The lash whistled through the air and a white-hot line of pain sprang up across my shoulder blades. My back arched of its own accord and I bit my lip to keep from hollering.

'Two dozen lashes, minus two,' Wilson intoned, and the whip sang through the air again. And again.

After a while, I didn't care that I hollered.

And then I didn't care about anything.

CHAPTER 15

I was out cold when Jerry Simpson laid me on a jail-cell cot, but I woke up right smart when he poured whiskey on my whipped back.

'Damn you. You don't have to pour lye on my back.' It hurt and I swore. Then Jerry went after my back with a rag and a basin of water. 'God a' mighty!'

'The whiskey'll kill any screw worms you mighta got from blowflies,' he said. 'I'll give you another dose after I get you cleaned up. You got some dirt and rocks in them cuts somehow.' Simpson worked gentle for a big man. The cuts on my back hurt like the devil, but the pain was nothing compared to Wilson's slashing bullwhip.

'That's as good as I can do, Ness,' Simpson said. 'I'm gonna give 'er another sloshing with the whiskey now.' He poured 80-proof fire all over my back, and I almost passed out again. Then he laid a clean flour sack over my back. 'I done what I could, Sheriff,' he said to Hubbell. 'But Ness Havelock's a hard man. He'll be up before long.'

I heard Hubbell coming toward me. 'You feel strong enough to talk, Ness? I need to hear your end of what happened. Harlow Wilson's told his version for the whole town. Like as not, a mob'll be after your hide, or what's left of it.'

I turned on my side and tried to get comfortable. Then I told him the whole of it – the Norwegians on Cotton Creek, the Mogollon Land and Mining Company, how Wilson had sent word to Roland Prince, and how I found him dead and Ace Cruger dying.

'What I can't figure,' I said, 'is why Wilson and his riders were on the road to the RP Connected instead of taking the fork toward Saint Johns. I don't put much stock in happenstance.'

'Dark out now,' Hubbell said, peering toward the high window. 'Don't think Wilson will get 'em whipped up tonight. You might as well sleep on it.'

'If you need help, Sheriff, you can talk to Sid Lyle. He's a good man with a gun and he'll stand. Them four who ride with him may help, too.'

'Yeah. Jim Houck's out after that Swingle kid and I sent George Creaghe over to Show Low. Funny how deputies are always gone when you need 'em most. See you *mañana*, Ness. I'll get Jerry Simpson to watch things while I'm out.' Hubbell stepped away.

I grunted and turned my face to the wall. The whiskey smart was gone from the whip slashes and the cotton flour sack lay light on my back. Sleep would have been a good thing, but I kept thinking about how things were piling up hereabout. Then Margarita Pilar wormed her way into my head with her warm smile and golden skin. I'd promised to care for her and here I was, whipped bloody, lying in a cell, and maybe facing a noose.

Somewhere along the line I slept.

The sun rose on another clear, bright Arizona summer day. Light poured through the window in the back of the four-cell jail. Simpson came in, surrounded by the smell of crisp-fried bacon and toasted sourdough bread.

'Can you sit up, Ness?'

'I can,' I said, and levered myself upright to sit on the edge of the cot. Simpson hooked the cell door open with a boot and brought in a plate piled high with bacon, fried eggs, buttered sourdough toast, and boiled potatoes sliced cold and fried golden brown in bacon grease. He dragged a chair in and set the plate on it.

'You eat,' he ordered, and handed me a fork.

I piled in. The food tasted mighty good, even to a man facing a hanging. I was on a second slice of toast and forking potatoes into my mouth when my brother Garet and his friend Tom Morgan, a tall black man who had a hook in place of his right hand, walked in.

'What's this about you killing Roland Prince?' Garet demanded. He'd ridden too long as a lawman to let serious things like murder slide. So I told my story again.

'And I still can't figure out what Wilson and those Pitchfork boys were doing in that neck of the woods,' I said. 'Could be they had something to do with the ambush that got Roland and Ace.'

'I reckon Ness will have to tell his story to Judge Westover,' Sheriff Hubbell said from the door. 'The judge's due through here in a week or so. But we may have a problem keeping Ness from a hanging party. A bunch of rowdies were at the Longhorn last night. Baldy Fontelle was buying drinks like he's just found the mother lode, and going on about how Ness had shot his own friend, and how he oughta hang. I reckon we can expect trouble.'

A man couldn't enjoy his breakfast to that kind of talk. I pushed the remains away and got a second cup of coffee.

'Hubbell, you want to deputize me? I'll stand against any rowdies,' Garet said. He would, too. He'd stopped a mob of miners cold in Vulture City when he was marshal there.

'I'll stand, too, Sheriff,' Sid Lyle said from the front door. 'And I got four good men.

Ain't nobody gonna take Ness outa that cell while we're here.'

'For a man who took a shot at me, you're all-fired loyal, Sid.' I grinned.

He grinned back. 'Mistake,' he said.

'All right,' Hubbell said. 'Garet, Lyle, raise your right hands.' Hubbell swore them in as Apache County deputy sheriffs and gave them each a badge.

'Sheriff,' Garet said, 'likely they'll come tonight. You go about your business and me and Sid will make sure Ness stays safe until the judge shows up. We'll just keep the badges outa sight for now. That OK with you?'

My big brother never ordered anybody to do a thing. He'd always say what he thought should be done and then asked everyone if his plan was all right. Mostly they agreed, but sometimes someone had a way of making the plan better, and Garet always welcomed the best way to do things.

Simpson took the breakfast tray away. Then came the sound of running horses and clattering wheels. Garet automatically palmed his Colt and Tom Morgan shifted his weight to bring his big Ballard .50 into his hand. Sid's gun was out, too. A sweating team pulled up in front but I couldn't see who it was.

'Am I some criminal that you should point your guns at me?' Rita demanded. Her voice was two degrees below freezing.

Garet and Sid looked embarrassed and holstered their six-guns. I couldn't help but grin.

Rita had a basket on her left arm. And she'd brought Old Mujer, the healer.

'I understand that you are holding a wounded and innocent man in your jail, *Señor* Sheriff,' she said to Hubbell. 'Of his innocence, I am positive,' she declared, 'and I brought Abuela to minister to his wounds.'

She brushed past Hubbell and paused in the doorway to speak to Garet. 'Thank you for sending Dan Travis from your Rancho H-Cross to tell me of Ness. And please tell Laura that I still live at Rancho Pilar, where she is always welcome.'

Garet touched a finger to the brim of his hat.

The two women marched into my little cell and took over.

'You, *señor.*' Rita looked at Jerry Simpson. 'Some hot water, *por favor.* Very hot.'

The old woman sat down on the pine floor and dumped powders into a pottery bowl and poured in a measure of oil. She worked at the lumpy mass with a wooden pestle. An aroma of herbs arose.

Jerry Simpson returned with a steaming kettle. He set it down and beat a retreat to the boardwalk.

'At least someone cleaned your back,' Rita

183

said, clipping her words. 'I have never known a man who could stumble into so much trouble, Ness Havelock. I labor to learn of herbs and medicines from Abuela, for I fear I will often have to take care of your many wounds.' Then, tenderly, she asked, 'Do you feel pain?'

'If I can take Simpson pouring whiskey all over my back, I can take anything Old Mujer can conjure up. I do need a shirt, though.'

'When Old Mujer has tended your poor back, *querido*, I will get you a shirt.'

'*Esta preparado*,' the old woman said.

Rita said, 'Turn on your stomach please.'

I lay on the bunk with the mincemeat of my back bared, while the old woman slathered her concoction up and down the raw slashes. 'What is that stuff?' I asked.

'Aloe, chamomile, clover, and elder bark, mixed with olive oil and wool grease,' Rita said. 'You need not wrinkle your nose, Abuela is wise in the ways of healing.'

The salve felt good, and seemed to pull the pain from the whip tracks.

'You will now lie still until Abuela's salve has time to go into your flesh. The herbs will remove the pain and help your body to heal.'

'The best thing for a wounded body is to get up and walk or work or do something,' I said.

'Johannes Havelock, you will listen to me.

Stay still, at least. Sleep if you can. Tomorrow is soon enough for moving around. *Comprende?*'

I lifted my head to look at her and my heart turned over. Her beauty astonished me. My chest tightened, and I found it hard to swallow. Then her eyes bored into mine and I could only nod my understanding.

'*Bueno*,' she said, her voice softening. 'You will sleep now, my Ness. I will watch.' She sat down on the chair that had recently held my breakfast, and folded her arms beneath her breasts. The old woman gathered up the tools of her trade and left. I hated to close my eyes and shut out the vision that sat beside me, but my eyelids drooped on their own and I slept.

I woke with a start when the front door crashed open.

'Someone's fired up the crowd over to the Longhorn, Sheriff,' Garet announced. 'Me and Sid had better start wearing badges. You got a shotgun?'

Rita backed against the bars of the cell, her eyes wide. 'Will they come for you, *querido?*' she asked.

'If someone buys enough booze and spreads enough rumor, some'd rather lynch a man than let him stand before a judge. They'll be coming all right.' I called to the sheriff and he came to the door.

'Be obliged if you'd get Miss Pilar out

185

before the mob gets here.'

'Come on, Miss Pilar. I'll take you to the Higgins House.'

'But I don't want to leave.'

'Like Ness says, this is no place for a woman right now.'

'Ness, I will not,' she said. 'Put your shirt on, Ness.' She held out a gray shirt that she must have gotten while I was asleep.

'Thanks. Now leave. Please.' I pulled on the shirt, which was a little big.

'What must I do to stay with you, Ness? Always you are sending me away, or going away yourself. Not once have you ever asked me to stay, to be with you, to stand by your side. Always it is go. Go. Go. Go.'

A tear rolled down her cheek. I wanted to reach out and gather her into my arms. But instead I said, 'Look at me, Rita. Tell you what you see. You see a rambler who has no place to call home. Not even a dugout. Nothing to show for all the years I've been riding. Nothing.'

'I do not care to see what you own, Ness Havelock. I see a man who rode from El Paso when his brother needed him. This same man came from Utah when a friend called. I hear the blacksmith has hired a new helper, a Norway man introduced by Ness Havelock, who helps people from somewhere far away. You have much, Ness Havelock, because you have much to give.

That is the man I see. And I only wish that he would give of himself to me.'

'Rita, this jail is no place for you to get stubborn. Men who want me dead are gonna come stomping down that street, lusting for my blood. You mean more to me than I can put into words, but I can't let you stay. Now please go.'

'Oh, Ness.'

'Go.'

Hubbell poked his head in. 'Ness, we'd better get her outa here.'

She stood, tears streaming. 'I will find it very hard to forgive you, Ness Havelock, for sending me away yet again.'

'We'll find time for forgiving later. Now go.'

She swept from the cell and through the door.

'I'll see that she's safe, Ness.' Hubbell followed her.

Rita was gone. I ached for her. I hadn't kissed her, though I couldn't forget the kiss she'd given me the night I rode from Rancho Pilar. I might never get another.

But, if this was to be the end of me, perhaps it was just as well, for her sake.

CHAPTER 16

The double-throated roar of a shotgun cut through the rumble of the drunken mob as they arrived in front of the sheriff's office.

'Hubbell, we know you've got that no-good Ness Havelock in there,' Baldy Fontelle shouted from the midst of the crowd. 'We want him.'

Sheriff Hubbell stepped out to face the milling men.

'Yeah,' hollered a drunk. 'Nesslock's got to pay for what he did to them fellers he kilt. What was their names, Jess?'

'Prince and Cruger,' shouted another slurred voice.

'Yeah, them fellers was good ol' boys, they was. Let us in and we'll give Nesslock what for, we will.'

Garet Havelock stepped on to the boardwalk to stand at Hubbell's side, the star pinned to his vest catching the light. Sid Lyle flanked the sheriff on the other side.

'Take a hard look at your hole card, gents,' Hubbell said. 'This here's Deputy Garet Havelock. Used to be marshal at Vulture City. And this other deputy's Sid Lyle, late of El Paso. And look on the roofs around.

We got plenty of help.'

The crowd went silent. From above came the sound of Winchester levers jacking shells into rifle chambers.

'Harlow Wilson has accused Ness Havelock of killing Roland Prince and Ace Cruger. Maybe he did; maybe he didn't. Ain't for me to say. But Havelock ain't leaving my jail until Judge Westover gets here to hold a trial.'

'We're all the jury that ranny needs,' Fontelle hollered. 'Hand him over, Hubbell, and save the county the cost of a trial.'

'Junior Willis,' Hubbell called to a silhouetted gunman on a roof across the street. 'The gent in the white hat that just hollered is Baldy Fontelle. Them boys try to rush us, and you shoot Fontelle first, you hear?'

'Got a bead on him right now, Sheriff,' Willis responded.

'Now, boys,' Hubbell said, 'you can see there's no point in pursuing this. I've got you covered from all sides. Just look around.' Peering around, the agitated men saw three men standing across the street, sawn-off shotguns in the crooks of their arms. Further along the street, more hard men watched the murmuring crowd over the barrels of their Winchesters. And from the corner of the bank building, Tom Morgan took aim with his Ballard .50.

Men in the back of the crowd started

peeling away, and minutes later, the mob was only a memory.

I spent most of a week in the sheriff's holding cell, sleeping a lot and eating three meals a day. Whoever was on watch brought the food, Garet or Sid and once even Tom Morgan. But Rita stayed away.

'Judge Westover's due in tomorrow, Ness,' Sheriff Hubbell said. 'When he gets set, we can clear things up.'

'You know my end of it,' I said. 'Don't reckon there's much evidence though. The way those Pitchfork men stirred things up, I doubt there's much of anything left there.'

'We sent Tom Morgan out to have a look. He may find something.'

'I don't know nothing about Judge Westover or courts or any of that. I've shot men in self-defense, but not Roland, and not Ace.'

'From what I've seen,' said Hubbell, 'the truth usually comes out. 'Specially when Judge Westover's doing the asking. He's a stern man, and justice is his trade.'

'I've got a bad feeling about this,' I said. 'Somewhere along the line, someone dealt me a worthless hand.'

'Ness, you've got more people on your side than you'd think. Don't you be getting down on yourself.'

'So when's the hearing?'

'Day after tomorrow, I'd reckon.'

'Not that I don't appreciate your hospitality, Sheriff, but I'm getting mighty tired of these bars. About now, I'd like to be looking at the backside of the Wasatch Range on my way to Wyoming.'

'Wilson brought the complaint, Ness. I gotta hold you.'

'I know. But I don't have to like it.'

A week had done a lot for my striped back. The lacerated skin had healed over and the deeper slashes had hard scabs on them. They were nothing to keep me from riding, and Gatlin's bullet hole in my side gave me no more than a twitch once in a while.

'Where's my buckskin, by the way?'

'Livery stable. He's getting fat and sassy on county oats.'

What would I do if things went like Wilson wanted? I couldn't imagine getting hanged without a fight, but would Garet and the others stand by me? Would there be a way to get free?

Sid Lyle came in with the evening meal, beans and beef, but I sent the food back. That night I didn't sleep much either. I'd shut my eyes and Rita would be sitting there telling me how she would not soon forgive me for sending her away. I wanted to see her real bad.

While a breakfast of eggs and bacon and sourdough biscuits didn't whet my appetite much, I forced myself to eat some.

Just before noon I heard a rap on the front door, and a great bass voice rumbling in the office. A minute later, Sheriff Hubbell came into the cellblock leading a huge round man. 'This here's Judge Westover,' he said.

'So you're Johannes Havelock,' the judge said. 'I always like to see the defendant before he's in the dock. Hmmm.' His deep voice seemed to echo in the great cavern of his chest.

'Judge Westover?' I started to state my case, but the judge held up a hand.

'Arguments come when the hearing's in session, son. You'll get to have your say.'

'But Judge–'

'Are you hard of hearing, young man?' The deep voice turned stern.

'No sir, but–'

'No buts.' He turned to the sheriff. 'Have this man at the schoolhouse by nine tomorrow morning.' Not waiting for an answer, Judge Westover strode from the cellblock, leaving me to wonder what the visit was all about. One thing about him, though, he wouldn't stand folks talking back. And he went by the rules.

Garet came in a few minutes later. He hauled up a chair and sat outside the bars.

'Any word from Tom?' I asked.

'He ain't back yet. But if there's anything out there, he'll find it. He didn't spend ten years with the Jicarilla Apaches for nothing.'

'I'd say Ace and Roland were shot with .44 or .45 caliber bullets. Sure wasn't no buffalo gun ... but I guess that's no use to me.'

'The hearing ain't over yet, Ness. Let's go a step at a time.'

'I got no mind to hang for killings I didn't do, Garet.'

'I know. But this country's getting civilized, Ness, and that means following the law.'

'I been thinking a lot while I sat here for a week. Whereabouts in Texas is Harlow Wilson supposed to be from? Where are his fifty thousand cows? Why's he keep orphan boys at the Pitchfork? And why'd he whip that boy Ronnie Dunne to death? Garet, there's lots about that man that don't set straight. I wonder if anyone's ever checked him out in Texas? I swear, if there's one man·in this territory who's got no business accusing me of murder, it's Harlow Wilson.'

'Wilson's riding high, Ness. He's in with the merchants who call themselves the Saint Johns Ring. Folks think he'll bring lots of money to town.'

'That just makes me wonder where those cows are. And where's he plan to run those dogies?'

'This is a hell of a time to be bringing this up, Ness. Judge Westover's starting your hearing tomorrow.'

'I guess the judge coming in here told me I'm looking down the barrel of a cannon, and Harlow Wilson's set to pull the lanyard and blow my guts from here to Sunday.'

'Time's short, Ness. All I can do is have a stab at it.'

'Thanks, Garet.'

I thought about the fix I was in for a long time after my brother left. Pacing the little cell did no good. Damn, it was a long day. Damn, I wished Rita would come. Damn. Damn. Damn.

I kicked off my boots and lay down on the cot, hands behind my head. Slowly the daylight faded.

'You want some light, Ness?' Sid Lyle asked.

'Sid, you're a Texas man. You ever heard of Harlow Wilson or the Pitchfork brand around your neck of the woods?'

'Texas is an awful big place, Ness. No, I ain't heard of Wilson before coming here, but that don't mean nothing.'

'Fifty thousand's a lots of cow critters. You'd think there'd be some noise on the Trail, if nowhere else. You know Gus Snyder?'

'Wouldn't call him a friend, but I know him.'

'Could you get one of your boys to ride over to Round Valley and find out what Gus knows about Wilson? Tell him the Havelocks want to know.'

'Kid Kilgallen could do it. He knows Gus's bunch pretty well. What you got in mind, Ness?'

'I don't know, Sid. But something ain't right about Wilson. And he's trying to get me killed, legal or illegal.'

'Sorry about Moab, Ness,' Lyle said.

'I don't hold that against you, Sid, but if you'd get the Kid to riding, I'd be obliged.'

Sid Lyle left, and I was alone with my thoughts again. In the morning, I had to stand before that mountain of a judge and tell him I didn't kill Roland Prince or Ace Cruger, and I had no way to prove what I said. My thoughts roiled and the dawn came before I could get to sleep.

'Get your boots on, Ness. It's time to go.' Hubbell said from the doorway.

The time had come already. And me with no defense but my word.

CHAPTER 17

After Baldy Fontelle told the Wilson version of how I'd killed Roland and Ace, Judge Westover called me up. I didn't like standing before a judge manacled, but I couldn't do nothing about it.

'Do you give me your word to tell the truth, Mr Havelock?'

'Yes, sir.'

'Tell me what happened.'

I began telling my story, leaving out the part about the Norwegian pilgrims on Cotton Creek because I figured this had nothing to do with them. I was almost through when I heard horses come up to the schoolhouse, and then Rita Pilar and Emilio Velasquez came in. I had to swallow hard before I could go on.

'Could I add one more thing, Judge?' I said.

'Certainly.'

'I buried a youngster named Ronnie Dunne in Mexican Hat. He was just a shaver, probably about ten. He came into my camp with his back cut to ribbons by a bullwhip. Folks there said Harlow Wilson tied the boy to a wagon wheel and whipped him for running away. So when the man who called himself Judge Harlow Wilson rode in looking for that boy, I wouldn't let him go. That night, the boy died. Now I've shot men, Judge, and some of them died. But every one of them was shooting at me and would have done me in if I hadn't got them first. But Judge, I would never use whip on man nor beast.'

I unbuttoned my shirt and shrugged it off my shoulders. A gasp went up from the people in the room. I turned so Judge Westover could see the healing criss-crosses put there by Wilson's lash.

'This is how Harlow Wilson treats people, Judge.'

'Mister Wilson. What have you to say for yourself?' Westover intoned.

Wilson raised his head and looked down his nose.

'You know, as I do, your honor, that those who err must be disciplined for their actions. The Dunne boy was incorrigible. It's a shame his frail constitution could not stand the punishment that matched his transgressions, but I was his foster father by law and could therefore discipline him as necessary.'

Judge Westover nodded.

Wilson kept talking. 'As for Havelock, I was outraged by what he had done–'

I very nearly leaped at Wilson, manacled as I was, furious over the death of that young boy, and I recalled the vow I'd made over Ronnie Dunne's grave.

Somehow, I managed to control my voice. 'Judge,' I said, speaking to Westover, 'me and Roland Prince go back a ways. Once in Sonora, he saved my life. Nigh a month ago, he sent word to me that he needed help, so I came a-running.'

Wilson broke in. 'Your honor, Havelock is a penniless drifter. And he's half Cherokee, I hear. Why are we listening to this red savage?'

I turned on Wilson. 'Wilson, I got one thing to say to you and the rest of the Saint Johns Ring that thinks like you. Money ain't the measure of a man. Nor is the color of his skin. It's how square a man is, how he treats his neighbors, what he does for his friends. Down in Ciudad Juarez, there's an old Mexican grandpa who said it best – the most precious thing you can give your friends is your time.'

Wilson snorted.

I remembered something else. 'Judge Westover, there's something else. Baldy Fontelle said my gun was warm when he took it from me, but he didn't do that. I turned my Colt over to Harlow Wilson, so Baldy couldn't know if it was hot or cold.'

Silence descended on the room, then a renewed murmur as Tom Morgan appeared at the door and beckoned to Garet, who got up and left.

'Mister Wilson, what about Mr Havelock's contention?' the judge asked.

'He was unconscious when we brought him to town, your honor. I don't think he remembers clearly,' Wilson said.

'You enjoyed laying your bullwhip to my back, Wilson, but you'd better not believe your whipping stunted my memory. Everything you did is carved into my head.'

Garet reappeared. 'Judge Westover, I know it's unusual, but my friend Tom Morgan has something to tell the court. Would you mind if he came in?'

'Has it bearing on this hearing?'

'Yes, sir.'

'Show him in.'

I sat down and waited for Tom to stand before the judge.

'State your name.'

'Thomas Jefferson Morgan.'

'Give me your word to tell the truth.'

'I do, sir. I don't cotton to liars.'

'Proceed.'

'Well, sir. I went out to where Mr Roland and Mr Ace was bushwhacked, sir. The ground was tore up good around where they was lying, so I scouted roundabouts. Took me a while to find 'em, Judge, but they was there.'

'Who was there?'

'Not *who*, Judge, *what*.' Tom Morgan held

199

out a big left hand. It held two empty brass shells.

Judge Westover took the shells. 'Hmmm. .44-40,' he said.

'Yes, sir. Someone laid under a juniper at the tree-line of the swale, Judge, and I'd say he shot Mr Roland and Mr Ace. He stamped those shells into the ground, but I still found them. To me, those cartridges say Ness Havelock didn't kill those men.'

Wilson jumped up. 'Judge Westover, I object. Who knows where that man got those shells? He may or may not have gone to the site of the killings. I can't believe he's telling the truth. Everyone here in Saint Johns knows he's obliged to Garet Havelock, brother of the accused. I think you should disregard this man's testimony.'

'Sit down, Mr Wilson.'

Wilson sat.

The crowd shifted at the back of the room, allowing Leif and Ellisif Hakansen to enter. The Norwegian couple walked resolutely forward to stand beside Tom Morgan.

Judge Westover raised an eyebrow.

'Sir. We do not speak your language good, but we want to say something.'

'Have you anything else to say, Mr Morgan?'

'By the sign, I'd say Roland Prince and Ace Cruger was shot from ambush by a Winchester .44-40, Judge. That's all I know.'

'You may stand down.' Westover turned his attention to the Harkansen couple. 'Now, sir, madam. May I ask your names?'

'I am Leif Hakansen, and this wife is Ellisif.'

'What business have you here?'

I could see that Leif was apprehensive, and I wondered why he'd walk into something he didn't know much about.

'Sir, do you say Ness Havelock – what do you say – murdered two men?'

'That is the reason we are here.'

'I, we, cannot believe that.' Pointing at Wilson, Leif said, 'That man brought us to here after we paid large monies. We were promised free land. But we got only four busted wagons and some old horses. We are fifty-three from Norway. We have a camp at the place called Cotton Creek.'

'Make your point,' Judge Westover demanded.

'No one helped us. No one. Except that man,' Leif said, pointing at me. 'He got Kort Bjornsen working at blacksmith. He got ten men helping Elijah Taylor's farm. Now we fix wagons and we have food. That man did such things for us, who are strangers.'

Leif took a step toward Judge Westover and leaned forward, speaking almost confidentially. 'Ness Havelock is not one who murders: we fifty-three say so.'

Wilson jumped to his feet. 'Your honor,

my people transported these pilgrims to Arizona as contracted. The ignorant peasants don't even speak English, except for this one. Surely you can't take what they say seriously.'

'This is a hearing, Mr Wilson. I listen to all. A man's character dictates what he does.' The judge drank from the glass of water on the table.

'Mister Hakansen, is that all you have to say?'

'Ness Havelock would not murder, sir.'

'Yes, yes. We heard your statement. You may go now,' Judge Westover said.

The couple worked their way through the crowd and wormed into a place against the far wall near Ruel Gatlin.

William Sessions shoved his notebook into a pocket and quietly left the room. A buzz followed the newspaperman's exit. He never left in the middle of anything. Where was he going? What was his hurry?

I appreciated folks speaking up for me, but what they said wouldn't prove I didn't shoot Roland and Ace. If the judge decided on a trial, Harlow Wilson would load the jury with men from the Saint Johns Ring and get me hanged.

I glanced at Rita, who stood just inside the door. She stared at the floor, but just sight of her beauty left me breathless. Emilio Velasquez was no longer there, and Rita was standing too close to Baldy Fontelle for my liking.

Judge Westover ignored the murmuring crowd as he wrote on a stack of paper. People started talking louder, and louder, but stopped the moment Bill Sessions returned. He walked straight to Judge Westover's table and laid a large envelope on it.

'Roland Prince came to my office a few days ago, your honor. He said this envelope was to be opened in case of his death. I'd neglected to do so, but thought there might be something in it important to this hearing. And here's a note Mr. Prince gave me when he came to my office.' Sessions pulled a folded scrap of paper from his pocket and handed it to the judge. 'He had been getting death threats and felt he might be killed.'

Judge Westover read the note, then opened the envelope. It held two sheets of paper and a bundle of death threats. Westover took his time reading the two sheets of paper. The crowd remained silent except for the odd cough or sniff.

At last, Judge Westover looked up. 'This concerns you, Mr. Havelock. It's Roland Prince's will.' He began to read.

'The last will and testament of Roland Prince.

'I, Roland Prince, being of sound mind and memory, do make this my last will and testament, written by my own hand this seventh day of July, the year of our Lord eighteen eighty-four. Item one: It is my will that upon my death my ranch, the RP Connected, as defined in the deed accompanying this document go to Johannes Havelock.'

A murmur ran through the room, and I guess the shock was plain on my face.

Judge Westover continued. 'Item two: Mr Harlow Wilson holds a ten-thousand-dollar note in my name. This money was borrowed on personal cognizance and represents no lien upon the RP Connected ranch. Nevertheless, it is my will that Ness Havelock sell enough cattle and property to pay Mr Wilson what is due.'

The judge paused. 'Is that true, Mr Wilson? Do you hold such a note?'

'Yes, your Honor.'

Judge Westover nodded.

'Item three: In that I have received threats to my life in the form of notes made of words cut from newspapers, if I meet an untimely death, I must assume that whoever sent said notes orchestrated my demise.'

The crowd rumbled again.

'Order,' said the judge. 'There is more.'

'Item four: It is my will that Johannes Havelock continue to employ those who work on the RP Connected, namely, Albert Ace Cruger, Kenigan Zane, Randolf Sandy Klieg, Timothy Montana Underwood, Evan Brown, and Snuffy Dagan, for at least one year from the date of my death. This is my last and final will and testament. Signed Roland Prince.'

Judge Westover surveyed the faces in the schoolhouse. 'This document was witnessed by Thomas Finney and Raymond Osgood. Would either of these gentlemen be with us today?'

A graying man in black broadcloth stood from a seat in the back. 'I'm Tom Finney, your honor.'

'Did you witness Roland Prince sign this document?'

'Me and Ray Osgood watched him sign the bottom of a paper, Judge, but he had it covered so we couldn't read what it was, but if my name and signature are on that will, I'd say it's what we saw him sign.'

'Thank you.'

Harlow Wilson sat sucking at his lower lip. I was still stunned. The judge picked up the bundle of notes and thumbed through them.

There was a commotion at the door, and Dan Smith struggled down the aisle on a pair of crutches. The foot I'd shot at Twelve-Mile Knoll was gone. Right behind him came Jim McCarty, Gus Snyder's Round Valley barkeep.

Judge Westover waited patiently for the two men to reach his table. I noticed Kid Kilgallen standing just outside the door, and knew that he'd brought McCarty, but why was Dan Smith here?

'Get this gentleman a chair,' said the judge, waving at Dan Smith.

'Have you gentlemen something to say to this hearing?' Judge Westover asked, after Smith was seated.

Jim McCarty spoke first. 'I tend bar in Round Valley, Judge, where Gus Snyder lives.'

Judge Westover's eyes narrowed at the mention of the outlaw leader's name, but he said nothing.

'Mister Snyder said to tell you, Judge, that he don't know any Harlow Wilson from Texas, but he says that Judge Roy Bean's got a warrant out for the arrest of a man named Wilson Baird. Seems Baird killed a man over a card game west of Pecos. Stakes were high and Baird got a note for ten thousand dollars, then killed the man he got the note from. Rumor has it Baird changed his name and came to Arizona.'

Wilson feigned indifference to what McCarty was saying, but the edges of his ears started to turn red.

'One more thing, Judge,' McCarty said. 'None of Mr Snyder's sources has heard a thing about fifty thousand cows. Mr Snyder says he'd wager there's no such thing as a Pitchfork herd.'

Wilson's ears got redder.

'Continue,' the judge.

Smith spoke. 'I reckon it's my turn. Just over two weeks ago, Judge, I rode with a bunch of Pitchfork men to Twelve-Mile Knoll. A couple of Mex sheepherders told us Ness Havelock was up there, so after Baldy Fontelle killed the herders, we went after Havelock. Our job was to kill him, Judge, and we tried. But Havelock was holed up and he got Pecos, shot me in the foot and hit Pete Petersen in the butt – excuse me, Judge.'

'Then why are you here?'

'Well, when Ness Havelock was making his getaway, he told me he'd send help. And, by God, he did. Baldy Fontelle and Rod Destain left me and Pete lyin' there, but Havelock sent help. That's why I'm here, Judge. I figure he saved my life, maybe I can do the same for him.'

Smith started digging something from his back pocket. He held it out to Westover. 'I thought you might want to see this, Judge. I got it from one of the kids at Pitchfork head-quarters.'

Judge Westover opened the yellowed news-paper. It was full of holes where someone had cut words out of it.

I heard Rita give a little scream. I whirled around and saw Baldy Fontelle with his Colt pressed to Rita's jaw. He had her arm twisted up behind her back.

207

'Boss!' Fontelle called, and Wilson surged to his feet.

Fontelle barked out orders. 'I want all the men to put their iron on the floor and kick it away, or the little lady gets a bullet.' He dug at Rita's throat with the muzzle of his six-gun. She flinched, her eyes wide with fear.

Sheriff Hubbell dropped his gun and kicked it away. 'Do what he says, folks,' Hubbell said.

Six-guns and rifles clattered to the floor and skittered across the wood as their owners kicked at them.

'Rod, get the guns off them outside,' Fontelle ordered.

Destain motioned the men inside, taking their hardware as they came in.

'Boss, we'd better be leaving. They're on to us,' Fontelle said.

Wilson nodded.

'Rod, you get out there with your saddle gun and shoot anyone that comes out the door, y'hear?' Destain positioned himself outside.

I noticed Ruel Gatlin in the corner. He was watching Baldy Fontelle the way a snake watches a rat.

Wilson reached into his coat, pulled out a folded piece of paper, and tore it in two.

'No use for the note on Roland Prince now,' he said, and laughed. He tossed the scraps of paper on the table in front of the judge as he turned on his heel and strode from the room.

Baldy Fontelle stood behind Rita. 'Anyone moves, this woman is dead. Just sit back and relax till we're out of sight. But just in case you get any ideas, I'm taking the girl along. If you come looking for us, she dies. Killing greasers don't bother me none.'

Rita's eyes found mine, but I couldn't do a thing.

Baldy Fontelle dragged her outside, hoisted her onto a saddled bay and the Pitchfork riders thundered out of Saint Johns.

CHAPTER 18

After Judge Westover ruled no trial, I wanted to ride after the Pitchfork kidnappers, but Sheriff Hubbell and Garet took forever getting supplies together. Finally we rode out two abreast with Tom Morgan leading. We had flour and sow belly and beans and coffee for four days, and with a hundred rounds for pistol and rifle each, we were loaded for bear and primed for killers.

Sid Lyle and me held our mounts to an easy lope as Tom and his rangy mule followed the trail left by Rita and Wilson's men. Junior Willis and Nate Blackthorn came behind us while Sheriff Hubbell and Garet rode rearguard.

Our horses were grain-fed and fit, ready for the chase, but with Wilson's long head start, we'd not soon catch up.

Sheriff Hubbell had found a dodger on Wilson Baird, also known as Harlow Wilson, wanted in Pecos, Texas, for murder. But he found nothing on Destain or Fontelle. Baldy killed Cesar Ramirez and Aldo, but no one had sworn out a complaint against him.

'There'll be shooting when we catch up to them,' Hubbell said, 'but we'll Injun upon them if we can. I don't want Miss Pilar hurt.'

He didn't want Rita hurt? I had to keep her safe, no matter what.

That night, we camped on a trickle of water in Gooseberry Wash, and ate saleratus biscuits and gravy made from flour and bacon grease.

'Me and Tom'll take first watch, if it's all right with you, Sheriff,' Garet said.

Hubbell nodded. 'Then I'll take the midnight watch with Junior, and Ness and Sid can take over at three or so. Nate, that puts you in charge of breakfast.'

Wrapped in my soogans, I listened to horses cropping grama grass, and next thing I knew the sheriff was shaking me.

'You awake?'

The night was black with no moon, and diamond-bright pinpricks of stars spread across the sky. I sat up and shook out my boots. 'Sid up?'

'Has been for an hour.'

Damn. I secured my bedroll and picked up my Winchester. I shoved a hand through my gunbelt and let the Colt hang at my side with the belt over my shoulder.

'Where do you want me?'

'I sat on that little rise just north of here. You can see pretty good from there.' The sheriff shucked his hardware and boots and got into his bedroll.

I walked to the top of the little knoll and

hunkered down. Listening to the night, I found myself remembering Rita, and the fear in her eyes as Fontelle dragged her from the schoolhouse, his cocked pistol shoved into the soft flesh beneath her jaw.

Suddenly I wanted to saddle Buck and ride after the bastard. Time was wasting. Rita and Fontelle were getting further away. But I stayed on watch till dawn.

When a streak of gray finally showed in the east, I went to camp and built a fire. While water heated in the coffee pot at the edge of the fire, I crushed a fistful of coffee beans with the butt of my pistol and dumped them in the pot. I sliced sowbelly into a skillet and soon had it sizzling. The sky lightened and the dark lumps on the ground turned into sleeping men. I forked the fried bacon onto a plate, broke cold biscuits in half, and put them face down in the skillet to warm. 'Bacon and biscuits,' I hollered. 'Come and get it.'

The sleepy posse gathered around, chewing on biscuits and slurping the hot coffee – hard men on a hard ride, and some might die before the end of this trail.

'Can't catch those murdering sons standing here,' Hubbell said. 'Let's move.'

Buck was more than ready to go and he pranced a bit as I swung up.

We hadn't been on the trail long when Tom, serving as scout, brought his mule loping back. 'I found somethin',' he said. He led us over a rise and into a swale where a yearling steer lay dead. Meat had been cut from its haunch, and its tongue was gone.

'They only stopped long enough to get meat,' Tom said. 'Probably kept movin' all night. By the sign, I'd say Fontelle's leading with the Pilar woman right behind. And someone on a lame horse came along here after the other four. Maybe we'll ride up on him first.'

But we didn't. He reached the Brewer place and traded mounts before we got there.

Giberly Brewer, an old man with a gap-toothed grin, met us with a rifle.

'Howdy, Brewer,' Hubbell said, his star in plain sight. 'We're on the trail of a woman and four men, one with no hair.'

'Couldn't say.'

'You seen 'em?'

'Nope.'

'Them's poor-looking horses in your corral.'

'They got run yesterday.'

The sound of a hammer on anvil came from behind the house.

'Shoeing?' the sheriff asked.

'One throwed a shoe. Come up lame.'

'How long's the man who come in here with that lame horse been gone?'

Brewer squinted at the sheriff, his eyes on the star. 'Now, Sheriff, I'm not saying nobody come here. But if they did, I'd say they got a couple hours' start on you.'

'What about the woman?' I asked.

Brewer shifted his squinty eyes in my direction. 'Dunno about no woman, son,' he said, 'but if I did, I'd say she wasn't enjoyin' herself. Nope. But I don't know nothin'. Nothin' at all.'

'She been gone long?' I asked.

'Well now, being as no woman come through here, I can't say that her and three men left before noon.'

'And you don't know where they was headed either.'

'Now that you mention it, son, I did hear sumpin' sounded like Me-hi-ko, and maybe it was Coranada and Hannagan. But I couldn't say, being as nobody come through hereabout, 'specially not no bald man with fire in his belly. No, ain't been nobody here.'

'Much obliged, Mr Brewer,' I said.

The old man gave me a gap-toothed grin. 'I gotta live with all kinds, son. I do what I can and what I gotta.'

We watered the horses and filled canteens from the creek that ambled through the Brewers' pasture.

'I'll bet on that bunch taking a beeline through Hannagan's Meadow to hit the Coronado Trail,' I said. 'They can follow it through the Chiracahua Mountains to Mexico.'

'That makes sense,' the sheriff said.

'They ain't gonna have a place to change mounts again,' Garet said. 'Let's push hard through the Boneyard and across the Prieta Plateau. That way we got a chance of heading them off at Cienega.'

'Them rannies ain't come through the cut yet,' Sheriff Hubbell said when we got to Cienega. 'We'll wait for 'em on the Hannagan's Meadow end.'

CHAPTER 19

'Now, we're not drygulchers,' Hubbell said. 'I don't want no one shooting before we give them Pitchfork people the chance to surrender. Understood?'

'Not that they gave Roland and Ace any warning,' I said.

'Ness, we don't know who killed Prince and Cruger, but we're not here to do any cold-blooded killing, and you know it.' The sheriff's voice held a sharp edge, and I knew I'd spoken outa turn. But I didn't apologize. My friend Roland Prince was dead and in my mind Harlow Wilson did it, whether he pulled the trigger or not.

'You call the shots, Sheriff,' Garet said, to ease the tension.

Hubbell continued, 'Now, there's seven of us and five of them, counting the woman. We'll hunker down on both sides of the cut, and they may well listen to reason.'

With no more than a couple of hours of daylight left, Rod Destain rode toward the cut with Wilson on his heels.

Sheriff Hubbell stepped onto the trail. 'You're surrounded, Wilson,' he called. 'Give up.'

216

Destain jerked his Colt and fired. The sheriff's leg crumpled from under him, and he fell among the rocks at the bottom of the cut.

I had a bead on Destain, but he whirled his gray mare as I pulled the trigger and my shot went wide. Gunfire came from across the cut where Sid Lyle and Nate Blackthorn hid. Wilson's horse collapsed, kicking and screaming, dumping the big man among the boulders. He scrambled for cover.

Destain's horse plunged into the trees with bullets clipping branches left and right around its rider's ears.

Then silence. The gunsmoke gradually cleared. Wilson stayed behind his boulder. I heard a horse scrambling for the top of the ridge. Someone was going over.

'Sheriff,' I called out, 'you catch lead?'

'In the leg, Ness,' he answered. 'I'm all right.'

The boom of Tom Morgan's big Ballard echoed off the western heights, followed by a scream and the sound of a body falling through tree limbs. Then Destain's panicked voice, 'Shit! Oh, shit, oh shit–' His riderless gray mare clattered by Wilson's dead horse and loped south through the cut.

No sign of Gatlin. No Fontelle. No Rita.

I made my way to Sheriff Hubbell, slipping from rock to tree and keeping an eye on Wilson, who remained motionless behind a big rock. As I neared Hubbell, something moved along the cut, and I ducked behind a log. A shadow flickered and Garet materialized. He'd changed his boots for moccasins, and he could almost touch the rock where Wilson cowered.

The sheriff held a bandanna to his leg.

'Let me see that,' I said.

Hubbell took his hand away. Destain's bullet had plowed through the outside of his upper thigh, cutting his britches like a knife and slicing through a good three inches of flesh, a clean furrow with just a trickle of blood.

I pulled out my clasp knife and cut a bigger hole in his britches, then refolded the bandanna and slapped it back on the wound. The sheriff jumped.

'Damn you, Ness. Be gentle with a man's sore leg, would you?'

I chuckled. 'Just a big of scratch, Sheriff. You'll be ready to ride bulls in the roundup rodeo by fall.' I took off my own bandanna and used it to tie the pad in place. 'But it's still a long ride home.'

'Yeah. Now give me a hand up.'

I'd pulled Hubbell to his feet.

'Sheriff?' It was Garet.

'I hear you.'

'Wilson don't want to fight. He's ready to go back to Saint Johns and wait for Roy Bean's marshal.' Garet waved Sid Lyle and

218

the others in, but Tom Morgan stayed high up on the west ridge.

'Look what's coming!' Sid Lyle said at the tree-line. Rod Destain stood leaning against a big pine, his shirt and vest torn and bloody at the left shoulder, and blood dripped from his slack fingers. He stretched a hand toward us, fingers spread wide. Then he went to his knees.

'Help me.' Destain's call was little more than a whisper. Then his eyes rolled back in his head, and he fell face down on the pine needles.

'Come on, Sid,' Garet said, 'Let's see what we can do for him.' The two tall men walked toward Destain's still form, one dressed in black, the other in old jeans and cowhide vest. They knelt over Destain. 'Ness,' Garet called. 'Bring that medicine bag from my saddle-bags, would you?'

They'd turned Destain over by the time I got there. The big slug from Morgan's Ballard .50 had caught him at the point of his shoulder, ranged down through the joint and shattered his shoulder blade on the way out. If Destain made it, his left arm would never be of much use.

Garet cut away the shirt, exposing the huge exit wound. He took muslin from the bag, made a six-inch pad, and put it over the wound. The pad was soon soaked with blood. He stacked another pad on top of it, and another. He bound them tightly to Destain's shoulder and torso with muslin strips.

'How's he look?' Sheriff Hubbell asked.

'We'll have to haul him on a travois, Sheriff. He'll live, maybe.' Garet hollered at the others. 'Nate. Junior. Could you boys catch that gray mare? We'll need her to get Destain outa here.' The two Claymore riders mounted up and trotted their horses down the cut after the mare.

Wilson sat on a rock with his head bowed and his shoulders slumped, no longer the big man who'd roared into my camp near Mexican Hat.

'Wilson Baird,' Sheriff Hubbell said. He pulled a wanted flier from his vest pocket. 'I'm arresting you and holding you for the murder of Charles Hardesty of Pecos, Texas.'

I wanted Harlow Wilson to hang or to go to prison for the rest of his life. 'You can add the murder of Ronny Dunne to that, Sheriff,' I said. 'I'll swear to it.'

'OK, Ness. Swear out the complaint back in Saint Johns.'

'Ness Havelock!' Baldy Fontelle's roar echoed from the walls of the cut. 'Ness Havelock, I say!'

'I hear you, Fontelle.'

'Call that man off the mountain.'

'He'll come down when he wants.'

Baldy Fontelle rode into view. He held a manila rope that ended in a noose around Rita Pilar's neck. In the same hand, his pistol was cocked and digging deep into her soft flesh. By reflex, my hand went toward the butt of my Colt.

'Don't even think about it, Havelock.' The web of Fontelle's thumb held back the hammer of his Colt while his index finger pressed the trigger.

I knew I could shoot his eyes out, but I couldn't risk it. If he released his grip, the Colt's hammer would fall and a .45 caliber bullet would go up through Rita's throat and take off the top of her head.

I moved my hand away from my gun.

Fontelle smirked. He stopped the horses less than forty feet away. 'Now, you all just unbuckle your gunbelts and drop 'em on the ground.'

We stood there.

Fontelle jammed the pistol harder into Rita's throat. She tensed but her face held no expression. Her eyes were blank and she seemed to stare at the horizon. I searched her face, but she would not look at me. And I heard her words again – *it will be a long time, Johannes Havelock, before I forgive you for sending me away.*

I unbuckled my gunbelt and let it drop. The others did the same.

'Call the Negro.'

Garet complied. 'Tom,' he shouted. 'Leave him go. You can't take him without killing the girl.'

The Ballard roared and a pine branch fell inches from Fontelle's head.

'I see he heard you,' Fontelle sneered.

'Baldy Fontelle,' I warned, 'you'll answer to me.'

My eyes sought Rita's. Though Fontelle's pistol forced her head into an uncomfortable position, she looked at me. *I'll be there, Rita,* my eyes said. *I'll bring you home.* Slowly, her eyelids closed, then opened again. I knew she'd understood.

Fontelle gigged his horse forward and Rita's went along. As he came alongside me, he said, 'This woman's not yours, Havelock, she's mine. She's my protection all the way to Mexico, and beyond. You're the only one with reason to come after me, and you're scared of hurting her. There you have it, Havelock. I'll see you in Hell.'

'Baldy, take me with you,' Wilson begged, jumping up and standing in front of Fontelle's horse.

Fontelle stared at him. 'Get out of my sight, Wilson. You're nothing but bad luck.' He lifted a foot from the stirrup and shoved Wilson in the chest, sending him stumbling back onto the rocks.

Just then the sound of horses clanging over the rocky trail came from the cut.

Fontelle drew up, putting Rita between him and the oncoming riders.

'Tell 'em, Havelock. It's her life.'

'Nate! Junior!' I warned. 'Ride in easy.'

Nate and Junior appeared, leading the gray mare.

'Just keep on coming, boys,' Fontelle said. 'And keep your hands clear of them guns.'

Nate glanced at Sid Lyle, but Sid shook his head. The Claymore riders, hands on their saddle horns, almost brushed Rita's horse as they passed.

'Now, get off those nags and drop your gunbelts.'

Nate and Junior took their time getting off, but they complied.

I was sore tempted to dive for my .44, but I knew that even as I shot Baldy Fontelle, Rita would die. I ground my teeth.

Fontelle laughed as he walked the two horses down the cut. The pistol barrel beneath Rita's jaw forced her head back, but she made no sound.

'Ness Havelock,' Fontelle called back. 'Don't try anything between here and Mexico, or the woman's a goner.'

I couldn't help answering. 'Baldy, you're a dead man. Wherever you go, I'll be after you. Keep looking back, 'cause I'll be there.'

Fontelle's laugh echoed long after he was out of sight.

Sheriff Hubbell started for his horse.

'Sheriff,' I said, 'I'm going after Fontelle, alone. If we all ride after him, we'll get Rita killed.'

I picked up my gunbelt, then waved Garet and Sid over. 'Garet,' I said to my brother, 'Roland Prince left me the RP Connected, but I've gotta go after Rita. Kenigan Zane is making a gather right now and, if you would, I'd like you to sell those cows. Then, if I'm not back by fall, have Zane round up everything he can and you sell them, too. Use the money to buy Herefords.

'Sid,' I said, 'if we get white-face cows, we won't have fights with the Claymore. You tell Preston Hanks what I've done. It'll ease his mind.'

Garet nodded, and I continued, 'Seven Mile Bend marks the property line between the RP Connected and the Pilar Grant at the Little Colorado. Could you take those Norwegian pilgrims over there and let them set up on the flats to the north? I think the bench north-west of Seven Mile Bend will farm fine. When I get back I'll deed them the land.' I grasped my brother's arm. 'Can you take care of that?'

'Ness, don't worry about the RP Connected. Go bring Rita back.'

Sheriff Hubbell pulled the wanted dodger from his vest. 'Ness, there's a five-hundred-dollar reward on Wilson Baird. I figure it's yours. I've got thirty-five dollars you can have. I'll get it back out of the reward money.'

'I got a hundred and fifty,' Sid said.

They all chipped in so I had $347 and most of the provisions.

'Big Brother,' I said as I swung up on Buck. 'I got one more favor to ask.'

'What's that, little Brother?'

'Drop by Rancho Pilar and tell Don Fernando I swear to keep my promise.'

Garet slapped me on the leg. 'Go to it, Ness. I'll tell him.'

The light was nearly gone when Buck came out of the cut and into the swale called Cienega. About three steps into the open, he pricked his ears toward the tree-line. Ruel Gatlin rode from the trees. Now was no time for a showdown with him.

'Gatlin,' I called, 'I know this has been a long time comin', but I'd take it kindly if you'd put our fight off a little longer.'

He grinned. Then I noticed his hands were on the saddle horn. 'Ness Havelock, you're a hard man,' he said. 'I figured you'd come riding after the lady.'

'That's what I'm doin'.'

'Then I'd like to ride along.'

CHAPTER 20

'If that cracker-ass roan can keep up, you come along,' I said, turned Buck's head south and lit out at a long lope. Gatlin's blue roan came right along after my buckskin like a blood brother.

After the sun went down and the dusk faded into night, we settled down to a walk. The roan stayed nose-to-flank with Buck for a while, then Gatlin brought him up alongside. 'Havelock,' he said, 'you're a hard man all right, but part of that hardness is in your head. What's your rush?'

I turned to peer through the dark at his square face. 'Fontelle's got a good head start. But I'm aiming to catch that varmint before another day's out.'

Gatlin clucked his tongue and wagged his head like I was a barefoot kid.

'You don't have to tag along, Gatlin. If Fontelle kills me, your job will be done and you can go home, wherever that is.'

I felt his hot gaze. 'My home's the back of this roan horse, or a chair in the local saloon,' he said. 'Never had none else since my brothers got killed up to Telluride.'

'Then why you ragging on me?'

'I don't want you dead. Not even by my own gun. Back there in Saint Johns, I seen you was a good man. They's too few good men, so I'd like to see you save your hide.'

I stared at Gatlin. 'I don't aim to die,' I said.

'But you keep on charging ahead like this and I'll guarantee you'll catch a slug. 'Course, if it hits you in the head, it'll likely ricochet.' He chuckled, and that took some of the fire out of my guts.

'You figure I'm gonna ride into one of Fontelle's bullets, eh? Well, he potted at me on Twelve-Mile Knoll and he didn't shoot all that straight.'

'Don't bank on that.'

We rode on without saying anything. Night sounds were normal. Crickets. The rustle of aspen leaves. The soft plop of our horses' hoofs. I took a deep breath of high mountain air, laden with the balsam taste of fir and spruce.

After a while he said, 'How did you take the Pitchfork Bunch?'

'You was there. We laid for them at the mouth of the cut to Cienega.'

'That's what Fontelle will do, too. He'll be lying up some place where he's got all the advantage. You ride in and he'll hit you blind.'

Gatlin had a point, but I didn't want to lose ground. 'We'll walk the horses all night.

Maybe rest a couple of hours before dawn. Don't want that jehu pulling away from us.'

'What about Miss Pilar?'

'What about her?'

'When it gets down to grits and gravy, what'll she do?'

The Rita Pilar I knew would bite and scratch, kick and scream, if she got half a chance. 'She'll make things hard for Fontelle,' I said, 'any way she can.'

Gatlin nodded.

We kept to the trail through the night. Then in the dark hours before dawn, we stopped to let the horses graze. We built a shield of aspen branches and made a hatful of fire to brew some coffee and heat bacon and biscuits.

As we rested, the world awoke. Camp jays flew in to look us over. A mule deer doe and her half-grown fawn crossed the meadow, then stopped to graze at the far edge near the trees. Thrushes twinkled in the brush, calling *tchup, tchup, tchup*. A gray tree squirrel with a russet line down his back flaunted his tail at us from the lowest branch of a big ponderosa pine. The brisk mountain air smelled of pine and fir and mountain grass crushed and cropped by our horses.

I filled our cups with the last of the coffee. 'It's about light enough to see if we can find some tracks.'

Gatlin nodded, pitched the dregs of his

coffee into the coals, and went to catch his hobbled horse. I whistled for Buck, and he came running for the oats I hand-fed him.

'Good trick,' Gatlin said, as he bridled the roan and threw blanket and saddle on its back.

'He knows he'll get something good if he comes,' I said.

Plenty of hoofprints on the trail, but I couldn't tell if Fontelle and Rita had made any of them. Fontelle said he was headed for Mexico, and at the moment, I had no reason to think different. We rode until the sun rose high and the flies bit hard, without finding any clear sign of Fontelle's passage. Then, as our shadows walked beneath us, Gatlin hollered, 'Havelock, come here.'

I gigged Buck over to where Gatlin sat his roan, fifty yards or so off the main trail. He pointed at a broken twig with a red thread clinging to it.

'Two horses took off eastward,' Gatlin said. 'Could be Fontelle and Miss Pilar.'

'I don't know how she managed to leave that sign,' I said, 'but I'm betting she did.' Then me and Buck trotted after the tracks.

Gatlin followed, and pretty soon he said, 'How 'bout we stop and look and maybe listen for a mite before crossing any meadows?'

For a youngster, he was a careful man. I hauled Buck to a stop. 'Gatlin, you just gave me a thought.' I got off and dug a pair of moccasins from my saddle-bags.

'What's the Injun boots for?' Gatlin asked.

I changed into the moccasins and climbed back on my horse. 'Got 'em from my Cherokee granddaddy,' I lied.

'Yeah. I'll bet.'

'OK, Gatlin. Here's your chance to keep me alive. When we get to a meadow, I'll hang back in the trees out of sight and you ride on like you was trying to catch up with Fontelle.' I grinned. 'You being an outlaw and all.'

Gatlin didn't look happy.

'If he shoots at you, I'll Injun around and get him. Us Cherokees can sneak up on any white man.'

After a while, he nodded. 'OK, I'll do it. We might as well start with that clearing up ahead.'

I stayed back in the trees while Gatlin loped the roan out into the meadow. Nothing happed. We repeated the Gatlin bait trick three more times and then, where the Blue and San Francisco rivers come together, we found a valley not more than a hundred yards across, flanked by walls of malpais twenty to thirty feet high. A stream flowed down the middle, fed by springs on the mountainside.

I got off Buck and bellied up to the tree-line to watch. The blue roan trotted with a springy step; nothing said he'd been going almost four days without a good rest. Some horse, that roan.

Gatlin rode with his hands crossed on the saddle horn. Suddenly dust spurted up from the trail in front of him, followed by the crack of a saddle gun.

'Hey, Gatlin,' Fontelle yelled. 'Where in Sam Hill you going?'

Gatlin calmly reined in the roan. 'Looking for you, Baldy,' he called. 'Wilson and Destain got caught by the posse, and you're the only one left.'

'Where 'bouts is Havelock?'

'Don't see him with me, do you?' Gatlin answered.

With my horse ground-hitched in the shadows, out of sight, I ghosted through the trees. Gatlin kept Fontelle talking, and I homed in on the bald man's voice.

'So how 'bout it, Baldy? You going to let me ride into Mexico with you? The law's still after me for shooting that card cheater in Casper. I need to get across the border.'

'Gatlin, you pulled a gun on me back up the trail. I have a hard time trusting a man who jerks iron on me,' Fontelle hollered.

'You was mistreating a woman, Baldy. Real men don't do that,' Gatlin replied.

Fontelle laughed.

As they jousted words, I Injuned around the tree-line till Fontelle was directly below me. Taking off my hat, I bellied up to the edge of the cliff and peeked down at Fontelle's fortress. Just as I got him in sight, he hollered, 'You mean this woman, Gatlin? Hell, she's just a Mex bitch.' He hauled off and kicked Rita, who was lying on the ground nearby, her hands tied behind her back. She cried out.

Gatlin slipped off the roan and gave it a slap on the rump. The horse bolted for the tree-line, and Gatlin took cover behind a jumble of malpais. 'Fontelle,' he yelled. 'I wanted to ride with you to Mexico, but I can't abide a man hurts a woman.' Gatlin fired at Fontelle's hideout. His bullet smacked into the malpais wall behind the outlaw and spattered him with rock chips.

'Damn you, Gatlin. What you so fired up about? She's just a Mex!'

Rita had worn the rope on her wrists through by rubbing the manila against the rough malpais. Fontelle fired at Gatlin, and as his rifle roared, Rita jumped to her feet and fled, dodging in and out among the malpais spires like a frightened cottontail.

I clawed for the .44 on my hip. Rita darted into the meadow and ran toward Gatlin. Fontelle's saddle gun roared and Rita went down with a scream, and lay still. For a moment everything in front of my eyes went black.

'Fontelle!' I screeched, and triggered the

Colt as fast as I could ear back the hammer. But I was too riled to shoot straight. Fontelle, that demon from Hell, sprinted for his horse.

My .44 held only empty shells, so I ran along the rim above him, then took a flying leap. My body crashed into him, knocking him off his feet and into the malpais. His rifle twisted away and bounced down the rocks to land on the meadow grass.

His rank unwashed odor got me really mad. He tried for his short gun, but I squashed his lips against his teeth with a right cross. I jammed him against the malpais, crushing his body into the rocks with my own. I had a grip on his gun hand that kept him from using the revolver while I pounded his face. Still, Fontelle managed to drag the short gun from its holster and struggled to cock the hammer.

'Fontelle, you murdering bastard,' I screamed. I knew I had to kill him. I cracked his gun hand against the malpais, sending the revolver clattering down the rocks to join the rifle. Then I began to beat him. Fontelle tried to fight, but my grief and hatred gave me extra strength. He went to his knees and covered his head and face with his arms. I kicked him in the stomach.

'Hey, Havelock!' Gatlin's voice broke through the red haze of my fury. 'Miss Pilar's OK. Just a scratch.'

I stood back. Rita was alive! I turned and saw her standing beside Gatlin, looking wan, frightened, and very tired. I started toward her. Fontelle slithered away and jumped on the spotted broomtail he'd gotten at Brewer's place. Bareback and hunched low over the cayuse's neck, he lurched into a gallop toward the south end of the little valley. I plunged down the rocky incline, whistling for Buck as I went. The buckskin came at a run. Fontelle was about halfway to the tree-line when I swung up and gigged Buck after him.

'Take care of Rita,' I hollered to Gatlin.

The buckskin ran. By the time Fontelle reached the treeline where he had to slow down, Buck had his nose to the tail of that spotted horse. Buck was a cutting horse and no more'n a dozen yards into the pines he was abreast Fontelle's paint. Buck took the west side of a big ponderosa while the paint went to the east. As the horses came together south of the tree, I jumped Fontelle, knocking him cross-body into another pine tree. The wind ooffed out of him, and he crumpled on the carpet of dead pine needles. I hauled him up by his shirt front and bashed him full on the jaw. He went down, struggling for breath. I punched him again, and again, taking skin off my knuckles. Fontelle finally went down to stay.

I whistled Buck over, pulled a pigging

string off the saddle, and used it to tie Fontelle's hands behind his back. Moaning in pain, he rubbed at the blood on his face with the point of his shoulder.

'Get on the paint, Fontelle. We're going back.' My words surprised even me. I'd been dead sure I'd kill the bastard, but there I was trussing him up like a prime roast and getting ready to haul him back to Saint Johns.

We made our way up the meadow and as we neared, I could see Gatlin had built a fire next to the malpais wall, and the smell of Arbuckle's wafted on the slight breeze.

'Coffee smells good,' I said, as we rode in.

Rita stood by the fire, her hair and clothes disheveled, her cheeks smudged with streaks of dirt, and a handkerchief bandage tied around her left forearm. Tears welled in her dark eyes as she faced me. I took her in my arms.

'Oh, Rita, thank God you're safe. I thought I'd lost you.' I held her, and she clung to me.

'Took you long enough,' Gatlin quipped. 'Go to a dance or something?'

I released Rita then, embarrassed by the mist in my own eyes. I sucked at my skinned knuckles. 'Yeah, sure. Some dance.'

He jerked his head at Fontelle. 'What's with the live bait? I thought you were gonna be judge and executioner for that bad-ass.

Begging your pardon, Miss Pilar.'

Rita smiled.

'The country's growing up, Gatlin,' I said. 'The law's got to rule if we want it to grow right. I could take my revenge on Fontelle here and now, but I'm going to haul him back to Saint Johns and turn him over to Sheriff Hubbell. We'll see what a jury says.'

I handed the reins of Fontelle's horse to Gatlin. 'Would you mind saddling this bronc and making sure he's delivered to the sheriff?'

Gatlin grinned. 'Nothing I'd like better than for him to try make a break. I can always say the deputy shot him.'

While I saddled Rita's horse, she stood holding on to its bridle. I knew I had to ask her.

'Rita,' I said, 'Roland Prince willed me his RP Connected ranch. I want to make good with that ranch, but not alone.' Gathering my courage, I plunged on. 'I was wondering... I mean, I'd sure be mighty pleased if you...' Then I finally got it out. 'Rita, would you consider being my partner?'

Her soft smile was like sunshine. 'Of course, Johannes Havelock. Of course I will.'

She threw her arms around me. And of course we sealed the bargain with a kiss that a man couldn't easily forget.

236

The publishers hope that this book has given you enjoyable reading. Large Print Books are especially designed to be as easy to see and hold as possible. If you wish a complete list of our books please ask at your local library or write directly to:

Dales Large Print Books
Magna House, Long Preston,
Skipton, North Yorkshire.
BD23 4ND